ET CETERA

ET CETERA

A COLLECTION
&c

By

AUGUSTINE BIRRELL

'On a log
Expiring Frog'

*From a poem by Mrs Leo Hunter
preserved in the
Posthumous Papers of the Pickwick Club*

Essay Index Reprint Series

 BOOKS FOR LIBRARIES PRESS
FREEPORT, NEW YORK

First Published 1930
Reprinted 1971

Library of Congress Cataloging in Publication Data

Birrell, Augustine, 1850-1933.
  Et cetera.
  (Essay index reprint series)
  Reprint of the 1941 ed.
  Essays.
  I. Title.
PR4115.E8 1971   824'.8   72-167310
ISBN 0-8369-2453-3

PRINTED IN THE UNITED STATES OF AMERICA
BY
NEW WORLD BOOK MANUFACTURING CO., INC.
HALLANDALE, FLORIDA 33009

CONTENTS

		PAGE
I.	A FEW WARNING WORDS FOR WOULD-BE AUTOBIOGRAPHERS	3
II.	BOSWELL DISROBED!	13
III.	THE PROVINCE OF THE REVIEWER DETERMINED	49
IV.	THE BIOGRAPHER OF SIR WALTER SCOTT	75
V.	JOHN WYCLIF	85
VI.	JOHN BUNYAN	97
VII.	GEORGE WHITEFIELD	117
VIII.	DR. CODEX	131
IX.	DR. DODDRIDGE	141
X.	CLERGYMEN AND CHURCHWARDENS IN THE EIGHTEENTH CENTURY	165
XI.	THE BIRTHPLACE OF 'PAMELA' AND 'CLARISSA'	189
XII.	NATHANIEL HAWTHORNE	199
XIII.	'NO CRABB, NO CHRISTMAS'	225
XIV.	THOMAS LOVE PEACOCK	233
XV.	HICKEY	241
XVI.	A CHURCH UNCHURCHED	269

I

A FEW WARNING WORDS
FOR
WOULD-BE AUTOBIOGRAPHERS

I

A FEW WARNING WORDS FOR WOULD-BE AUTOBIOGRAPHERS

I HAVE been in my time a great reader of Biographies—but am so no longer; for in my old age I have grown both tired and suspicious of biographers. The progress of somebody else's life told by somebody else, when you have grown somewhat weary of your own, has lost its old interest; the very headings of the chapters, intended to indicate the too familiar passage from the cradle to the grave, beget an impatience that compels one to turn the pages hastily in order to feast our eyes upon the welcome words 'Last Days'.

But why not be one's own Biographer? After so many years of scribbling, however lightly, on all sorts of subjects, until exhaustion has crept in, why not, in the hours of lassitude, turn your tired pen upon Yourself? You must know just a little more about yourself than ever you did about the Reformation.

If modesty forbids, as it well may, immediate publication, a type-written copy placed where it is not likely to be overlooked alongside of your last Testament, will spare your blushes, and at all events prevent anyone else from chopping you into chapters, and from quoting *his* (not your) favourite tags of poetry at the beginning of each of them, and from otherwise 'presenting' what he took to be 'You' to that sardonic, or frivolous fraction of the 'reading public' who direct the circulating libraries to keep them well supplied with recent 'Lives'.

After all, there is no novelty in the idea. Autobiographies abound! I once set out to make a list of those that surround me as I write, and though I had not the patience to make the list complete, I soon found that I had on what book-collectors smugly call 'their shelves', the autobiographies of Actors, Artists, Authors, and Astrologers; Clowns, Courtiers, and Courtesans; Editors and Egoists; Historians and Hangmen; Impostors, Invalids, and Infidels; Lawyers; Parsons, Poets, Painters, Philanthropists, Politicians, Profligates, Publishers and Prize-fighters; Rebels, and Radical Reformers; Soldiers, Sailors, Scholars, Saints and Sinners; and so on all down the alphabet.

If anyone therefore is bent, for want of other occupation, on writing an Autobiography, he or she will find on my list a precedent.

Fielding in the first chapter of *Joseph Andrews*, observes somewhat too caustically that Colley Cibber was thought by many to have lived the

WOULD-BE AUTOBIOGRAPHERS

strange life he did simply in order to be able to write it. If this be true, the best excuse that can be found for such a life as Cibber's is the delightful Autobiography it produced.

But if an Autobiography is readable it requires no excuse from the Reader's point of view.

Yet for all that, and notwithstanding their number, to write an Autobiography is a dangerous enterprise, and no wise man or woman should engage upon it without first counting the cost.

Sir Leslie Stephen, *Ultimus Romanorum*, in a passage of haunting significance, credits autobiographies with a peculiar charm, for, says he:—

'An Autobiography alone of all books may be more valuable in proportion to the amount of misrepresentation which it contains. We do not wonder when a man gives a false character to his neighbour, but it is always curious to see how a man continues to present a false testimonial to himself. It is pleasant to be admitted behind the scenes, and to trace the growth of that singular phantom, which like the spectre of the Brocken, is the man's own shadow cast upon the colossal and distorted mists of memory.'

Studies in Biography, III. 237.

'Curious', 'Pleasant'—but for whom? The reader or the autobiographer? No more devastating passage was ever penned since Swift. Could books read, there would be a disturbance in that corner of the library where these 'singular phantoms' cast their shadows. Though I have had these words by heart for years, they have never ceased to make me shudder—and now, their Author, one of the sincerest of men, stands like the angel with the flaming sword on the very threshold of the would-be Autobiographer, warning him off the course, for who would wish to become one of those 'singular phantoms', or to spend his last days composing 'a false testimonial' to himself?

If it be asked, how can the reader, who is sometimes a simple soul, ever come to be sure, or even to suspect, that the testimonial is a false one, or that the 'spectral figure' is not a true image, the answer is, and though it is (partly) my own, it savours of sublimity—by that Divinity that shapes our books, dictate them how we may.

An Autobiographer, however much of an artist, however delicate his embroidery, stands a very poor chance of deceiving even those of his readers who, coming long after him, never encountered the impostor in the flesh.

Autobiographers are woefully mistaken, if they believe they can act as masters of the ceremonial attendant upon their self-exposure, ushering their readers into one room, and excluding them from another. They can do nothing of the sort. If your frontage falls, the inside gapes. Would-be Autobiographers might

WOULD-BE AUTOBIOGRAPHERS

do worse than pause here for a moment, and read Browning's poem 'House' (*Pacchiarotto, and other Poems*, page 60).

It is strange how often men and women who write books forget all about the men and women who occasionally read them, a forgetful folly akin to that of the man who, having challenged a bruiser to engage in fisticuffs, lays down a plan of attack, but forgets to remember that his opponent is not likely to stand still all the time. Nowadays many readers are at least as clever as most authors.

Mr. Herbert Spencer, as stupendous an Egoist as Robert Southey, though he never wrote anything half so good as the 'Story of the Three Bears' in the latter's *Doctor*, appears to have composed his colossal memoirs on the supposition that his readers would be either 'automata', or befooled disciples, instead of being, as many readers of Autobiographies are, keen judges of character, disembowelled critics, and those who after long training in the art, craft or mystery of 'reading between the lines', have become not only skilled, but alert, to prick the bubbles of self-complacency, and to discern, only too quickly, the familiar indications of a congenital conceit, lurking clumsily beneath a mask of modesty.

There is no escape from this. Every book, wise

or foolish, cunning or simple, reveals the Author, not as he thinks he is, or wishes to be thought he was—but for all that, the Author. John Bunyan in his *Grace Abounding* thought he was revealing a hardened sinner, destined to the pit, saved from hell by a miracle of Grace, but what he does reveal is a loving tender-hearted man who from the first had all the tokens of a conscience-stricken saint; and this despite a picturesque vocabulary that was to make the fortune of *The Pilgrim's Progress*, and perhaps no great aversion from being on a friendly footing with the female members of his congregation. It did not need much of a miracle to convert John Bunyan.

How many Autobiographies are books of good faith? No one can give a convincing answer to this question. Artists in words are almost bound to create false impressions, and Dullards too often are conspicuously untruthful. Still, when there is good faith, evidence of it is continually cropping up. I feel as safe in the company of Montaigne as I do whilst reading on a Sunday night the sermons of Bishop Butler. Neither Montaigne nor Butler would (of this I am certain) wittingly deceive me.

All this to show the perils of the voyage! Anyone who begins writing about himself runs a risk beyond that of his publishers; for, self-

WOULD-BE AUTOBIOGRAPHERS

deluded as he may be about his character, or however skilful he thinks he has been in concealing it—out the truth will come. His best chance of escape is to have no character at all. But then?—

Nor can the Autobiographer escape detection by taking cover behind 'Important Events of Public Interest', with which he may stuff his pages, or by raising a false scent with the names of 'Personages', with which he may bespatter them, for in an Autobiography the main fact in issue is the Autobiographer. He it is after whom the hounds will run, and he it is they will eventually pull down, dissect and devour.

Here, I am stopped by familiar voices, loud and shrill, crying out 'For heaven's sake leave off prosing about character! Who cares about character? We want to be told about other people's characters, the men and women you have met either round the council table or at meat, men and women *alors célèbres*! Serve them up for us, repeat or invent their repartees, hint not obscurely at their mutual dislikes; remind us of their discomfitures in politics, love and war; and if you do this, and at the same time supply a good index, enabling us quickly to ascertain which of our friends, not to say ourselves, are mentioned in your records, why then you may die at your leisure, having discharged to our

A FEW WARNING WORDS

satisfaction and that of the evening papers the whole duty of an Autobiographer.'

This vain babblement, however, falls very flat on the ear of a man who has learnt in his own library the difference between one book and another. Unless a book reveals a character behind it, good or bad, it is a thing of naught.

Do you wish your real character to be self-revealed? If so, try your hand at an Autobiography.

II

BOSWELL DISROBED!

II

BOSWELL DISROBED!

THOUGH it may be true that in 1791 Boswell's two quartos of his *Life of Johnson* fell somewhat flat, and did not at once displace the authoritative biography of Johnson's Executor, the 'unclubbable' Hawkins; now, after many a cheerful day, *Boswell's Johnson*, like Homer's *Iliad*, has reigned supreme in its own realm, and has become one of the books it is superfluous, not to say tedious, to praise.

Amongst the ambitions of Boswell's life, and he was the greediest of mortals, the proudest was, to use his own boastful words, 'to Johnsonize the world'; and he has succeeded so well as to have become for most ordinary reading folk 'Johnson's Boswell', a kind of penumbra of the Great Bear. But to-day, after nearly one hundred and forty years, it would appear there is a good chance of another of his ambitions being realized, and that from this day forth he may, if not shine, at least shimmer in his own light as 'James Boswell Esquire'.

To fix the precise date when Boswell first succeeded in Johnsonizing the World of Letters might be difficult.

BOSWELL DISROBED!

In the later years, the post-pension years, of Johnson's life, Johnson had become the hero of a clique composed of famous men and quick-witted women, among whom he was '*Primus inter pares*'. The parting scene between Burke and Johnson makes it all plain to us even at this distance of time. Affection predominates the scene. Johnson captured the hearts of his friends more than their heads, and it is by a series of casual friendly sayings of his, recorded carelessly by Boswell and others, that he sways our memories and rules us from his urn.

Oliver Goldsmith in the course of his ramshackle, disorderly and troubled existence wrote wiser and more original things, and said not a few, than ever Johnson wrote or said, and yet Goldsmith, great man as he was, must always be content to remain *Ursa Minor*.

The coolness with which Boswell's Great Biography was received need surprise no one. It was original, outspoken, and expensive. The wise Mr. Pitt once restrained the prosecuting ardour of an illiterate Attorney-General, whose fingers were itching to put Godwin in the dock for his *Political Justice*, by remarking that a book costing three guineas was not likely to stir the mob. And let it be remembered there are always two mobs, one well- and the other ill-dressed, and neither book-buyers.

BOSWELL DISROBED!

Johnson, despite his occasional lodging in Mr. Thrale's fine new house in Grosvenor Square, remained to the end a dingy denizen of Fleet Street and the Inner Temple Lane, and to be invited to drink tea with Mrs. Williams can never have been much of an outing. We can easily perceive in Horace Walpole's contemptuous judgment 'the cold disdain' of the World of Fashion.

'Have you got Boswell's most enormous book? The best thing in it is a *bon mot* of Lord Pembroke's. The more one learns of Johnson, the more preposterous assemblage he appears, of strong sense, of the lowest bigotry and prejudice, of pride, brutality, fretfulness and vanity; and Boswell is the ape of most of his faults without a grain of his sense. It is the story of a mountebank and his Zany.'

This judgment, which I daresay still recommends itself to many a man of fashion, was not passed upon the *Life*, but upon the *Tour in the Highlands* with Dr. Johnson. When six years later the two volumes of the *Life* came into Walpole's hands, he at once wrote to Miss Berry, telling her he would report upon them when he had got through with them, and when he did make his report it was an unfavourable one.

Nevertheless, sneer as we may at the dullness of contemporaries, and always bearing in mind that Walpole was in Johnson's presence only six times, and then never interchanged a word with him, still, so far as it goes, Walpole has an advantage over those of us who, despite all our reading and raving about Johnson, never once stood in the same room with him.

But I am not going to alter my opinion about anybody at the bidding of Horace Walpole. Fashionable opinion counts for nothing in the lifetime of a book, and even in 1791 Johnson's friends and backers were a host in themselves. There was no better living judge of Literature than Burke, who went about telling everybody he met that in his opinion Boswell's *Life* was a greater monument to Johnson's fame than all his writings put together. (See *The Diary of a Lover of Literature*, 1810, p. 129.)

That admirable man, Edmund Malone, the best friend Boswell ever had, though, as will hereafter be noticed, a most inefficient Trustee of his last Will and Testament, brought out in 1799, after Boswell's death, the Third, and in my opinion, for reading purposes, the best Edition of the *Life of Johnson* in four volumes. From the appearance of this Edition the great popularity of the book may plausibly be dated. In the homes of our grandfathers or great-grandfathers, or in their ships on the broad seas, these four volumes were often more treasured than any others, and who can wonder?

BOSWELL DISROBED!

Whether Croker's much advertised, soundly abused, and wisely modified Edition, that after long delay appeared in 1831, added to the popularity of the Biography may be doubtful, but certainly it increased its circulation. Publicity even a hundred years ago availed much, and John Murray, with the *Quarterly Review* behind his back, was a great Publisher. On the other hand the personal unpopularity of Croker was as certain a fact as the good looks of Mr. Canning, or the essential greatness of the Duke of Wellington.

Anyhow, Croker's Edition made more noise in 1831 than the original had done in 1791. Macaulay fell upon it at once with a savagery he had long nursed, for he hated Croker more than he did cold boiled veal, the Sunday joint of his early Christian Clapham home; whilst a little later, in *Fraser's Magazine*, Carlyle cut Croker into pieces after an even more effective fashion. Both these Reviews, in the collected works of these two famous Reviewers, are still read annually by hundreds—an unusual fate for Reviews.

Everybody knows Macaulay's paradox. The Biography of Johnson is the greatest of English biographies, because its Author was the biggest Fool amongst Biographers. None the less, when Macaulay was induced to leave off despitefully using Croker, and forgot Boswell, his description of the Hero of the piece is such a downright, healthy, hearty bit of English as to have carried the name and fame of *Boswell's Johnson* to the uttermost ends of our Empire.

It is foolish to attempt to move Macaulay on. There he is, and there he will remain, blocking up the landscape, and at the same time adorning it.

Carlyle's review of Croker's Edition belongs to another order, yet I expect if poor Bozzy could have been consulted he would have preferred being called a Fool by Macaulay than to have sat for his portrait to the Author of *Sartor Resartus*.

'In that cocked nose, cocked partly as in triumph over his weaker fellow-creatures, partly to snuff up the smell of coming pleasure and scent it from afar; in those bag-cheeks hanging like half-filled wineskins, still able to contain more; in that coarsely protruded shelf-mouth, that fat dew-lapped chin—in all this who sees not sensuality, pretension, boisterous imbecility?—the under part of Boswell's face is of a low, almost brutish character.'

Here is a picture beyond Raeburn! The portrait of a Scottish Laird drawn by the son of a Scotch peasant who had been turned out, like 'auld Davie Deans' from his holding.

Carlyle's paradox seems almost as ridiculous as Macaulay's. But Reviewers of genius usually provide themselves with a way out, and Carlyle found his through the port-hole of his theory of Hero Worship. It was Boswell's *reverence* for Johnson that changed 'a foolish inflated creature, swimming in an element of self-conceit', into 'a real martyr to this high everlasting truth'.

In these non-moral days, we do not mind very much how Boswell, who was, no doubt, very much of a Fool, and a good bit of a Hero Worshipper, managed to write so magnificent a book. We know now that he took enormous pains over it, quite as much as Carlyle did with his horrible *Frederick the Great*.

Since 1831 Boswell has been edited and re-edited, how often we cannot stop to inquire.

Dr. Birkbeck Hill's annotated edition (though a rival Editor has picked some holes in it) stands to-day at the head of the list, though there are those who, sharing Johnson's opinion that 'Notes are necessary evils', when reading Boswell for pleasure, and not for the purpose of retailing recently acquired information, prefer to hold in their hands either Malone's Edition or the one we owe to Mr. Napier and his wife.

All this time I am shooting very wide of my mark, and have been writing under the shadow of the shield of the greater Ajax, Johnson himself. I must get out of the shadow, and think not of him but of Boswell, who now, after a very long last, stands a fair chance of standing before us.

'naked and unashamed', or as we have put it more delicately, completely disrobed.

Nor need we feel any delicacy in thus surveying him. Delicacy and Boswell have nothing to do with one another, and never had. Matthew Arnold's 'Adolescens Leo' of the *Daily Telegraph*, had indeed, so at least we are told in *Friendship's Garland*, once heard of the word. 'Delicacy', said he, 'Delicacy, surely I have heard the word before.' 'Yes,' he went on dreamily, 'in my fresh enthusiastic youth, before I knew Sala, before I wrote for that infernal paper.' But though Boswell's youth was fresh and enthusiastic enough he had never heard of the word, and it is only by a series of extraordinary mischances that this process of disrobing has taken so unconscionably long a time. Boswell cannot be blamed for this. So long as he lived he was always trying his hardest to disencumber himself of his last garment, He not only preserved almost every letter he had received, and kept a copy of almost every letter he had ever written, but when he came to die, it was found he had bequeathed all his papers to three of his most valued friends for the benefit of his younger children.

But before entering upon this posthumous revelation, and before explaining how it is that this avalanche of *Boswelliana* has descended upon our heads, and has escaped from its Babylonish

BOSWELL DISROBED!

captivity of more than a hundred years in an Irish castle, let us amuse ourselves for a few minutes in considering how Boswell himself began, when hardly out of his teens, undressing himself in public.

He began with an *Ode to Tragedy*, in sixteen ten-line stanzas, published in Edinburgh in 1761 (Boswell was born in 1744), price sixpence, and purporting to proceed from the pen of 'A Gentleman of Scotland'. This Ode, in itself a thing of no consequence, is dedicated in a prose address to 'James Boswell, Esquire', that is to Himself. In the course of this address he remarks that he would be sorry to contribute in any degree to the Author of the Ode acquiring 'an excess of self-sufficiency' and proceeds as follows:—

'I own indeed that when I have boasted of a glimpse of regard from the finest eyes and most amiable heart in the world, or to display my extensive erudition, have quoted Greek, Latin, and French sentences one after another with astonishing celerity; you, with a peculiar comic smile, have gently reminded me of *the importance of a man to himself*, and slyly left the room.'

This amazing bit of dedicatory impudence concludes after this fashion:—

'I must now bid you farewell, with an assurance that while you continue the man that you are, you shall ever find me with the greatest sincerity and affection,

'Yours, etc.'

My copy of this bit of nonsense was bought some forty years ago off a stall in Edinburgh for the published price of sixpence, and bears on its title-page, in Boswell's easily recognizable handwriting under 'A Gentleman of Scotland', *James Boswell, Esq.*, and below the 'price sixpence', the words *'dedicated to himself'*.

Except from the Author, and his friend Erskine, this Ode attracted no attention, and consequently remains one of the rarest of Boswell's early publications. I sometimes flatter myself mine is the only copy in existence, but probably I am mistaken about this. I usually am in such trifling matters.

Two years afterwards, in 1763, Boswell published, this time in London, *Letters between the Honourable Andrew Erskine and James Boswell Esquire.*

The prefatory note begins thus:—

'Curiosity is the most prevalent of all our passions, and the curiosity for reading letters is the most prevalent of all kinds of curiosity.'

The Letters themselves, so far as they are Boswell's, are ridiculous enough, but pleasantly reveal a characteristic of his, not given to many, yet in itself a most engaging one, that of being able to poke fun at himself.

I will give one quotation from the first letter in the book:—

'Auchinleck, *August* 25*th*, 1761.

'Dear Erskine,

'No ceremony I beseech you. Give me your hand. How is my honest Captain Andrew? How goes it with the elegant, gentle Lady ——? The lovely and sighing Lady J.? and how, O how does that glorious luminary Lady B.? You see I retain my usual volatility. The Boswells, you know, came over from Normandy with William the Conqueror, and some of us possess the spirit of our ancestors the French. I do for one. A pleasant spirit it is. *Vive la bagatelle* is the maxim. A light heart may bid defiance to fortune. And yet, Erskine, I must tell you that I have been a little pensive of late, amorously pensive, and disposed to read Shenstone's *Pastoral on Absence*, the tenderness and simplicity of which I greatly admire. A man who is in love is like a man who has got the toothache, he feels acute pain, while nobody pities him. In that situation I am at present, but well do I know, I will not be long so. So much for inconstancy.'

Mr. Tinker, in his fine recent Edition of *Boswell's Letters*, tells us that after 'long hesitation' he excluded the rather foolish letters to Andrew Erskine which Boswell wrote and published at

BOSWELL DISROBED!

the age of twenty-three, when he first aspired to a literary reputation'.

Foolish letters they most certainly are; Boswell seldom wrote anything in the shape of a letter that was not foolish.

But in parts they are not bad fooling, and occasionally very clever. Nor was Captain Erskine, his correspondent, by any means a dull dog. They were both great adepts at ridiculing one another. At the date of writing, Boswell was contemplating with fond complacency a career in the 'Guards', but shortly afterwards, on overhearing the free discourse of soldiers lately returned from the seat of war, his blood 'freezed within his bones', so that when he did go abroad, it was to study the Civil Law at Utrecht. It is to be feared that Boswell, unlike his eldest son, was always what is called a Coward.

The poetry with which the book is too full is not so good as the poetry in the *Arcadia*, and may be neglected, but as I have given a little bit of Boswell, it is only fair, even at this distance of time, to give the more gallant Captain 'a look in', particularly as in the passage selected there is a portrait of Boswell himself as he was in his twenty-third year.

'Since I saw you, I received a letter from Mr. D——: it is filled with encomiums upon you; he says there is a great deal of humility in your vanity, a great deal of tallness in your shortness, and a great deal of whiteness in your black complexion. He says there is a great deal of poetry in your prose, and a great deal of prose in your poetry. He says, as to your late publication, there is a great deal of Ode in your dedication, and a great deal of dedication in your Ode. It would amuse you to see how D—— keeps up this see-saw, which you'll remark has prodigious wit in it. He says there is a great deal of coat in your waistcoat, and a great deal of waistcoat in your coat, that there is a great deal of liveliness in your stupidity, and a great deal of stupidity in your liveliness, but to write you all he says would require more fuel in my grate than there is at present, and my fingers would be numbed, for there is a great deal of snow in this frost and a great deal of frost in this snow!'

How much of this belongs to Mr. D—— and how much to the Captain, who can say? Erskine was a younger son of a Scotch Earl, and his elder brother, who succeeded to the title as the Earl of Kellie, was that *rara avis in terris* a musical Peer. Andrew Erskine wrote a lyric, or one verse of a lyric, that was pronounced by no less a judge than Burns to be 'divine', but unhappily he took to 'card playing', and becoming 'frantic' after a run of bad luck, threw himself into the Forth and was drowned. Burns mourned over his death, and when writing about it said it had 'scared' him.

There is no necessity to refer to other early anonymous publications of Boswell's, though he never wrote anything that was not self-revealing, but I cannot pass over the book that at once secured him not the fame on which his heart was set, but that common substitute for it which he greedily devoured, Notoriety. In 1768, on the publication of his *Account of Corsica, the Journal of a Tour on that Island, and Memoirs of Pascal Paoli, by James Boswell Esquire*, Boswell at once became 'Corsica Boswell' and was soon able to write, 'I am really the great man now', and again after the Third Edition, 'I have obtained my desire, and whatever clouds may overcast my days, I can now walk here among the rocks and woods of my ancestors with an agreeable consciousness that I have done something worthy.'

The *Corsica* had a mixed reception. For the first time the 'reading public' began laughing at Boswell. It still continues to do so. What Walpole thought of Boswell's *Tour* we have already mentioned, but what did the poet Gray think about him, and his *Corsica*?

All that related to Paoli pleased and moved Gray strangely, but as for the *Account* he said it only proved 'what I have always maintained, that any fool may write a most valuable book by chance if he will only tell us what he heard and said with veracity. The title of this part of

BOSWELL DISROBED!

Boswell's work is a Dialogue between a Green Goose and a Hero!'

We now know that the *Life of Johnson* was not written by chance; or otherwise Gray might be quoted as being of the same opinion as Lord Macaulay.

But Boswell was quite satisfied with his notoriety, though much disturbed by the obstinate silence of his Mentor, the great Dr. Johnson, from whom he could extract no word of praise, and only one bit of advice, which was 'to empty your head of Corsica, which I think has filled it for too long'. Boswell's spirited reply is well known: 'Empty my head of Corsica? Empty it of honour, empty it of humanity, empty it of friendship, empty it of piety? No! While I live, Corsica, the cause of the brave islanders, shall ever employ much of my attention, shall ever interest me in the sincerest manner.'

After a bit, Johnson, yielding to pressure, went so far as to admit that though Boswell's History 'was just like other histories, copied from books', yet the Journal excited and gratified curiosity more than any other narrative Johnson could name. Then, but not till then, Boswell was made supremely happy.

Few people now read Boswell's *Corsica*, but his *Tour in the Hebrides* is so well known that it need only be mentioned as playing a part in this continued process of 'self-revelation'. The book contains other good things as well as Lord Pembroke's *bon mot*.

After the *Tour* in 1768 comes the *Life* in 1791, and the opinion might then well have been hazarded that Boswell's task of stripping himself naked before the world was completed, but as we shall now see, this was far from the case.

Boswell died in his London house in Great Portland Street on the 19th of January, 1795, and the report was soon widely spread that all his letters and papers had been destroyed. There was an end, so it might have been supposed, of the self-revelations of James Boswell, Esquire.

We must now jump from 1795 to 1857, when Mr. Bentley published a volume of Letters from James Boswell to the Rev. W. J. Temple, the grandfather of a late Archbishop of Canterbury.

The discovery of these letters is what, for want of the right word, we are condemned to call 'a Romance of Literature'.

In 1850, Major Stone of the East India Company's service in making a household purchase in Boulogne-sur-Mer, observed with the keen eye of a soldier that his parcel was wrapped up in a piece of wastepaper bearing the signature of James Boswell, nor did the gallant Major rest until he discovered that the paper came from the stores of an itinerant dealer whose habit it was to visit the shops of Boulogne to dispose of his wares. Then, marvellous to relate, the originals of the letters published in 1857 were found practically intact. Boswell being 'inimitable', there never was any question of their authenticity. Their appearance in Boulogne was explained by the fact that the eldest daughter of Mr. Temple had married an impecunious parson named Powlett (said to have been a grandson of Polly Peachum and the Duke of Bolton), whose necessities occasionally compelled him to reside in this neighbourhood.

In 1857 Boswell was a little 'out of the picture', and Bentley's venture, though well but anonymously edited by a grandson of *Junius*, and provided with an excellent Introduction, did not succeed in attracting the attention of 'indolent' reviewers and dropped out of circulation.

In 1908 the letters were reprinted with a new and equally admirable Introduction from the pen of the late Mr. Thomas Seccombe, an enthusiastic Johnsonian.

Eventually the originals of these Temple Letters were purchased, and now belong to Mr. Pierpont Morgan, who permitted Professor Tinker of Yale University to take copies of them and reprint them in his valuable collected edition of all the Letters of Boswell that he could then lay hands on, except, as aforesaid, the Erskine Letters, which he disregarded as not worth while. The Oxford Clarendon Press has published this collection in two handsome volumes, 1924.

We have thus three editions of the Temple Letters—1857, 1908, and 1924—and can, if we care to do so, combine the process of unveiling Boswell with the process of Bowdlerizing him. Boswell, it must be admitted, lends himself to this procedure. Yet it is hard upon him. He at least never wrote a letter without an eye to its publication. He wanted everybody to know everything about him; yet no sooner has a parcel of his intimate letters to a lifelong friend been almost miraculously rescued from the pastrycooks, than up jump creatures styling themselves Editors, and in their prudery, either their own or their publishers', claim the right to restore some of the garments of delicacy that the writer had discarded and cast to the winds.

Professor Tinker, the last Editor, tells us somewhat boastfully that having been allowed to make copies of the originals he is enabled to assure his readers that now, for the first time, they can read the letters as Boswell wrote them. This statement is not literally true, for the Professor goes on to admit 'that two or three phrases have appeared to me to be unprintable'. 'Two or three' is a vague phrase. Mr. Francis in 1857 found exactly six. There is not much difference. I have read in the Professor's Edition the passages that Francis omitted, and can truthfully report that I am neither the better nor the worse for the experience. We have not yet got a complete edition of Pepys. Some day it will appear. In the meantime, a complete unexpurgated Pepys is no argument for longevity. But is it not a little ludicrous for a man who takes upon himself the task of printing a collection of Boswell's Letters to lay down the law as to what is 'printable' or not? Boswell at his worst was not quite a John Wilkes; most of whose letters, save those delightful ones addressed to his natural daughter, have not yet succeeded in getting themselves past the printers.

In Professor Tinker's collection, Boswell can clearly be seen almost at full length, from head to heel, and in the Letters the reader will discern not only folly that would be almost incredible were it not under his hand and seal, drunkenness, melancholy, and degradation, but also strokes of humour, insight into character, and to a surprising extent, a humble recognition of the writer's infirmities and of his miserable shortcomings. As for his exuberant professions of piety, whilst I can recognize Boswell's cowardice, I will never call him a hypocrite.

It might well have been supposed that after Professor Tinker, the unclothing of Boswell was as complete as the Shaving of Shagpat, and that nothing remained for the onlookers to do but to cry aloud, with the innocent children in Hans Andersen's story of the 'Emperor's New Clothes', 'Why, he has got nothing on!'

But it has not been so ordained.

An avalanche of the Private Papers of James Boswell, who died in 1795, has descended upon us in 1928, to the amazement, almost to the bewilderment, of the great multitude, no man can now number, of Johnsonians and Boswellians.

This avalanche, though in size alarming, will break no heads and shatter no reputations.

But where have these papers been all this time? The answer is, in Malahide Castle in Ireland.

Some years ago rumours began to be afloat or, as the saying is, 'noised abroad' that in this picturesque castle, well known to Irish golfers, there were stowed away in an attic Boswellian treasures. I remember in 1907, when I was Chief Secretary to an Irish Lord-Lieutenant, under a now discarded regime, hearing such tales, but only to be assured by my authorities that the doors of the attic containing the papers were kept barred and bolted against all lovers of Dr. Johnson.

As a matter of fact, the last determined guardian of the attic and its Ebony Cabinet, and one who had watched over these papers with 'the efficiency of a Cerberus and the impenetrability of a Sphinx', was an old lady named Mrs. George Mounsey, *née* Boswell, who had died in 1906, and by her death the contents of the Ebony Cabinet had passed away to Boswell's great-great-grandson, the present Lord Talbot de Malahide. So, my authorities were, as authorities are apt to be, just a little behind the times. In 1907 the dragon was dead.

The Boswell Papers, released from their long captivity, are now in course of publication, though so far only for private circulation.

To explain how these Papers got across the Irish Channel, and why they were guarded so jealously, would be to write a history of the Boswell Family, and of their aversion, transmitted from one generation to another, to be identified with the scapegrace of their race. To a true Boswell there is nothing inexplicable in this.

Boswell's eldest son, Alexander, began the tradition, for as Sir Walter Scott told us long ago in a note to Croker's Edition, he was a proud man, and like his grandfather, the old Lord of Session (not of Parliament, as his son too often, when on his travels, vainly pretended) thought his father had lowered himself by his 'deferential suit and service' to Johnson. Alexander disliked any allusion to the *Life* or to Johnson himself, and, so Sir Walter goes on, 'I observed that Johnson's fine portrait by Reynolds was sent upstairs out of the sitting-room at Auchinleck'.

This note of Scott's in Croker's *Boswell* accounts for the references to Sir Alexander Boswell's animosity towards his father in Macaulay's famous, but on the whole mischievous, speech on Talfourd's Copyright Bill, 1841.

We are often required by novelists and playwrights to consider the differences between fathers, sons and grandsons, but was there ever such a catalogue of differences as those that existed between these three Boswells of Auchinleck? There was the father, the old-fashioned Presbyterian Covenanter, the hearty Hanoverian, the upright and sober Judge, who, though tried as few fathers ever have been by their sons, always treated his first-born with sound sense, generosity, and an amount of affection that excites our admiration, in both senses of the word. Then came the son of whom we know so much, who in his turn by some freak of nature begat Alexander; the gallant, the high-spirited Alexander, a gentleman, as the word was then understood, in every bone of his body, a man of the nicest honour, of whom an account may be read in Lockhart's *Life of Scott* (see vols. 4 and 5, pp. 159 and 179), but hardly without emotion.

Never before was so contrasted a triad!

Yet it is to the middle figure, the Boswell of

BOSWELL DISROBED!

Professor Tinker's *Letters*, that we owe as deep a sense of gratitude as we do almost to any human being.

The decisions of Lord Auchinleck are no longer cited in Edinburgh before the 'Fifteen', and he lives for most of us only in the famous retort he made to Dr. Johnson, which, having been recorded by Sir Walter Scott, is to be found in all annotated editions of Boswell's *Life*, whilst the lively pasquinades of the son Alexander that cost him his life in a duel, to say nothing of the song of his own composition 'Jeannie dang the Weever', which he sang one evening with such vivacity in Scott's house in Castle Street, Edinburgh, are now only dimly remembered by a handful of old men with both feet in the grave.

This family tradition begun by Alexander was handed down, year out and year in, until it perished in 1906 with Mrs. Mounsey. To put it all down to Scotch pride and 'Lairdism' is not a little unreasonable; there was that in James Boswell very hard for a descendant to stomach, nor can we forget that of all the Boswells the Biographer of Johnson was himself at once the proudest and the absurdest in his pride.

Boswell's will was written with his own hand and dated the 26th of May, 1785, and after even more than the usual protestations of piety and trust that he may be admitted to endless felicity in Heaven, appointed his long-suffering spouse, and his friend Sir William Forbes of Pitslico, Baronet, his executors, and then after many references to his entailed estates, proceeded to bequeath to Sir William Forbes, the Rev. Mr. Temple, and Edmund Malone, Esquire, 'all my manuscripts of my own composition and all my letters from various persons, to be published for the benefit of my younger children as they shall decide, that is to say, they are to have a discretionary power to publish more or less'.

After the testator's death his body was removed to Scotland and buried, as directed by his will, in the family vault at Auchinleck. A Memorial Tablet was suggested and a kindly epitaph composed by a relative prepared, but as the latter referred in its last line to both Johnson and Paoli, no memorial was ever erected by his sensitive descendants to the man who has made their name famous, or as they thought, infamous.

Boswell's eldest son, the aforesaid Alexander, succeeded to the estate, and married the eldest daughter of Sir William Eliott of Stoba and became the father of a son and three daughters. This son, strangely enough, was called James, and when his father came to his melancholy and premature death, lived at Auchinleck, and after marrying thedaughter of another baronet begat two daughters, and in 1850 began a legal process to prove the invalidity of the Auchinleck entail. The suit was contested by the next male heir, but succeeded, and Sir James Boswell was thus enabled to bequeath Auchinleck to his two daughters, Julia and Harriet.

Julia became the redoubtable Mrs. George Mounsey, and in her widowed state the dragon of the Irish castle, and Harriet married the eldest son of Lord Talbot de Malahide.

Returning now to the will of our James Boswell, what can be said about the remissness of his three literary executors and their disregard of their testator's wishes?

So far as the Rev. William Temple is concerned, we may assume he never took any trouble about his old friend's papers. He was far too harassed with his own affairs and a very large family[1] to bother about Boswell, nor had he long to live. But Sir William Forbes and Malone did at first bestir themselves, and exchanged letters on the subject, but after a while they decided to do nothing in regard to publication until Boswell's second son came to an age 'fit for selecting such of the papers as may be proper for the public eye'. This was a wise decision. There was no use in consulting Boswell's eldest son, for he would have consigned the papers to the flames, but

[1] See *The Diaries of William Johnston Temple*, Oxford, Clarendon Press, 1929.

BOSWELL DISROBED!

Boswell's second son, also a James, came of age in 1799, and was, one would have thought, the very man to be entrusted with the editorship of his father's remains. He lived in London the life of a scholar, collected books, and was the friend and first biographer of Malone. Somehow or another he did get hold of some of the papers, for when his library came to be sold in 1825 some twenty of the 'items' in the Sale Catalogue evidently had belonged to the father, including a MS. 'Common Place Book' entitled *Boswelliana*, which has been published in 1875 by the Grampian Club. This publication is preceded by the best biography ever written of James Boswell the Elder by Dr. Charles Rogers. No Johnsonian Library begins to be complete without this comparatively little-known volume.

James Boswell the Younger died in 1822, Edmund Malone in 1812, and Sir William Forbes in 1806. Nothing had been done with the Boswell Papers at Auchinleck, and they passed without notice into the possession of Alexander's son, Sir James Boswell, who, as already mentioned, died without male issue, but had managed to get rid of the family entail in favour of his two daughters. It is supposed that the papers were years afterwards removed from Scotland to Ireland by Lord Talbot de Malahide, the father of Harriet Boswell's husband, where they remained fiercely

BOSWELL DISROBED!

guarded by Mrs. George Mounsey, *née* Julia Boswell, who died in 1906.

These are the Papers, generally supposed to have been destroyed, that are now in course of private publication.

Some of the Papers have become totally illegible owing to damp, but none would seem to have been wilfully destroyed or removed, though I cannot but believe that the Biographer's son, James, a bookish man to the centre of his soul, borrowed other 'items' besides the Common Place Book and forgot to return them.

Six volumes of this private edition have already appeared under the judicious editorship of the late Mr. Geoffrey Scott, as we must now learn to describe him—magnificently printed books, but as they are not yet dedicated to the public, they cannot be pillaged by Reviewers, and I have only been permitted to see them by the kindness of my friend and brother bencher of the Inner Temple, Mr. Evan Charteris, who is the owner of a copy.[1]

But though I may not pillage I may state concisely, without quotations, the contents of these six volumes, all that is left hitherto unpublished of the literary wardrobe, the discarded garments, of the late James Boswell, Esquire.

[1] A copy has lately been presented to the London Library.

BOSWELL DISROBED!

The *First* volume of 'The Private Papers of James Boswell from Malahide Castle. In the Collection of Lieutenant-Colonel Isham and now first printed. Dedicated to the Memory of Edmund Malone', contains a General Introduction by Mr. Geoffrey Scott, and includes within its pages 'Early Papers' (1754–1763), 'A Journal of my Jaunt', 'Harvest' (1762) and 'The Oath of David Boswell'.

The *Second* volume (a most extraordinary one) contains 'Zelide', 'A Correspondence between James Boswell and Belle de Zeylen' (163 pages), 'Letters from Holland and from Lord Auchinleck', and 'The Inviolable Plan'.

The *Third* volume contains 'A Journal of a Tour through the Courts of Germany', 1764 (179 pages).

The *Fourth* volume is entitled 'Boswell with Rousseau and Voltaire' (152 pages), and, telling us as it does in Boswell's own words his incursions upon these world-famous men, presents, as Mr. Scott puts it, a spectacle 'of converging figures with an essential fitness and an exquisite incongruity'.

The *Fifth* volume, which like the others has an introductory preface by the able editor, contains the 'Love Letters' (in French) with a translation composed to divers Ladies of rank and fashion by Boswell, who, when in Italy, felt it a duty (how unlike Milton when in the same locality) to succumb to the prevailing atmosphere. Also his 'Journal in Italy'. The ladies, I am glad to say, held him at bay.

The *Sixth* and longest volume (291 pages) is entitled 'The Making of the Life of Johnson as shewn in Boswell's First Notes, Original Diaries, and Revised Drafts. A Study of Boswell's Biographical Method Marking the Successive Steps in the Composition'.

This volume, like its predecessors, is enriched and enlivened with facsimiles.

Here Mr. Scott's editorship was terminated by his untimely death. His little book or novelette, *Zelide*, written before he had seen the Papers he was destined to edit, proved how fitted he was by insight and critical perception for the task that was awaiting him.

Though there are other volumes to follow, yet so far as the 'Unveiling of Boswell' is concerned, the process, I am persuaded, is complete.

Here, the task I set myself being also completed, if I were well advised I might drop my tired pen, but I feel impelled to add something on my own account, and speak for myself about what are called 'Revelations'.

What right have we, the greedy public, to revel in revelations about dead people? Is it becoming, is it decent, to enjoy seeing them make fools of themselves, and to spend our spare time chuckling over their absurdities, not to say obscenities? Was not Mrs. George Mounsey, born Julia Boswell, the dragon of Malahide Castle, quite right in guarding so fiercely the 'Private Papers' of her great-grandfather? Nay! Would she not have done better had she made a bonfire of them and put them for ever out of the way? These are peevish questions, and I will leave the readers of Professor Tinker's Collection of Boswell's Letters and (when they get the chance) of these Six Volumes, to answer them for themselves.

For my own part, I steer as usual a middle course. Born in 1850, it would be idle for me to pretend to be anything else but a Mid-Victorian, a contemporary of the Prince Consort's Statue in South Kensington, and therefore one who still holds in reverence and godly fear the once familiar injunction 'Decency forbids'.

Yet, for all that, I make a Distinction. I cry *Distinguo*!

Everything depends upon the character of the man who stands revealed in all his nakedness, and the place he occupies in our memories.

Before National Heroes (and how few there are of them—shall we be generous and say half a dozen?), being of necessity men of valour, we bow our heads.

BOSWELL DISROBED!

Eloquence is now out of date, and even were it not, it is beyond my powers, but though I cannot produce it, I can borrow it, and it will answer my purpose.

'It is a thing most sorrowful, nay, shocking, to expose the fall of valour in the soul. Men may seem detestable as joint-stock companies and nations; knaves, fools and murderers these may be; men may have mean and meagre faces; but man in the ideal is so noble and so sparkling, such a grand and glowing creature, that over any ignominious blemish in him all his fellows should run to throw their costliest robes. That immaculate manliness we feel within ourselves, so far within us that it remains intact though all the outer character seem gone, bleeds with keenest anguish at the undraped spectacle of a valour-ruined man. Nor can piety itself at such a shameful sight completely stifle his upbraidings against the permitting stars.'

This outburst of eloquence flows from the pen that wrote *Moby Dick*, who though as a writer may be as unequal as George Borrow, is at least Lavengro's match in occasional spurts of inspired eloquence, almost as tremendous as the 'breathings' of his own White Whale.

It is, however, plain that our poor Bozzy cannot claim the benefit of Herman Melville's exception. Boswell was no Hero! no man of Valour. His was a character without Reserve! From the first he made a present of himself to the World, and took the greatest pains to preserve for posterity all the records of his shame. As one of his oldest friends said to him: 'Boswell, all men have their hobbies. Yours is Yourself'—and he might have added: 'you are riding it to death'.

A greater man than Melville has sought to establish another exception from defamation at the hands of Biographers and Editors of private papers.

In 1816 William Wordsworth, whose Poetry all men will now admit is of occasional magnificence, but whose Prose (when not imbedded in his Poetry) is always superbly excellent, published a letter to a friend on Robert Burns. In this letter Wordsworth deals with the question of Revelations with force and feeling, and denounces a particular Edinburgh Reviewer with a passionate indignation that would, to-day, bring him face to face with a Jury of London Publicans.

Wordsworth does not seem to mind very much about men 'who have borne an active part in the world'! *Their* private lives may, so he suggests, be scrutinized with 'some disregard of reserve', but he makes his exception in favour of Poets, for of them he says, 'if their works be good they contain within themselves all that is necessary to their being comprehended and relished'. And he goes on to say, very interestingly, that were he to hear 'On Boswellian lines' that records of Horace had been unearthed among the ruins of Herculaneum, he would not greatly rejoice.

Here again, Wordsworth is of no use for Boswell, who was no more a Poet than an heroic Soul.

The justification for the Boswellian Revelation must be based upon the fact of the character of the man. These Revelations after all tell us nothing about Boswell we did not either know before or might have guessed had we chosen.

Nobody will think any the worse of Lord Auchinleck's son or of Alexander's father because of these Revelations.

Indeed, it is just possible that among the younger generations (to which I do not belong) there may be some charitable souls who will like this poor Bozzy all the better for his unfailing candour.

It is not within most men's powers to be either Heroes or Poets, but it is very easy to be a Hypocrite, and Boswell most emphatically was not a Hypocrite; and may therefore take up his unrobed position in our Gallery of Notabilities without any feeling that he is intruding himself upon the company of his Betters.

III

THE PROVINCE OF THE REVIEWER DETERMINED

III

THE PROVINCE OF THE REVIEWER DETERMINED

Nothing is easier than to compose the Title-page of a Treatise like, for example, those of John Locke and John Austin. The difficulty begins when you attempt to elucidate your theme.

It is a mistake to compose the Title-page first and begin writing the Treatise afterwards. Your Title-page may get into your head and turn your brain.

Poets (and who would not be a Poet, if he could?) have made (we suspect) this blunder oftener than Prosemen.

The *Course of Time* by Robert Pollok was published for the first time in 1827. What a noble Title for a great Poem! A hundred years has not diminished its majesty. It still stirs even sluggish imaginations. Nor did it fail in 1827, though it was then the era of Scott and Campbell. Twenty editions were speedily demanded, and the Author, the most deserving of men, netted in cash the sum of £2,500! It was no doubt what is called a pious Poem, but why should piety be forbidden to twang the lyre or to cash a publisher's cheque?

After some years of declining popularity the *Course of Time* breathed its last in 1857, in the arms (if the expression is permissible) of one of the most splendid editions of a single Poem, of great length, that appeared in the last century. The proud Publishers (William Blackwood & Sons) said no more than the bare truth when they declared in a few modest prefatory words that the *Course of Time* had in this edition obtained 'the highest tribute a Publisher can bestow or which a Work can receive' in a form 'profusely illustrated by the best talent which the Art of Design can place at the service of Poetry'.

As to the profusion there was left no room for doubt, for the Wood Engravings, some designed by Tenniel and executed by Dalziel and others, were fifty-five in number! It was indeed a splendid affair.

> 'So past the strong heroic soul away.
> And when they buried him the little port
> Had seldom seen a costlier funeral.'

There is no need now, nor would this be the place, to say anything about the Poem itself, for the Author was all that was estimable as a man and died young—but it is hard to believe that in 1827, when distinguished poets abounded and were largely read, there could have existed in the land of Burns a young man capable of composing, and a Publisher capable of printing such lines as:—

> 'Hold my right hand, Almighty! and me teach
> To strike the lyre.'

Happily for me, my Title has nothing intoxicating about it. How could it have?—for it is borrowed from Austin's *Province of Jurisprudence Determined*, a work once held of high authority at the Examination Tables of the University of London, but now almost as much out of fashion as Pollok's *Course of Time*, though I admit it has not yet been published in an illustrated edition.

What then is the Province of a Reviewer 'properly so called'? What significance lies in the word Review? Has it any applicability to books of old renown, or has it now become confined to notices of new books or new editions of old books? Is 'Reviewing' a Profession or but an avocation for the curious, the idle, or the destitute? Can it pretend to be an Art, and if so can it be taught? That it entails duties must be assumed—but what are those duties?

These questions are easy to ask, nor are they very hard to answer—but not after a very appetizing fashion.

Many years ago I read in one of those Preliminary Dissertations that in the early part of the last century often formed the imposing and inviting Porticos to substantial volumes, Encyclopædias, and such like, that 'the origin of Reviewing has been attributed to Photius'.

In those days a hint so broad was never lost, and I set off at once in hot search of this Photius from whose entrails sprang the whole buzzing, stinging tribe of Reviewers. At first, I started on a wrong scent and found myself reading about a Photius who was a son, by a former alliance, of that very wicked woman the Empresss Theodora, in whose career, as one might expect, Gibbon took so unholy an interest. This Photius was consequently the stepson of Justinian, whose *Institutes* have played so considerable a part in the early education of many Reviewers, who little thought it was to be their destiny to become Reviewers.

The stepson of Justinian proved not to be the man I was after. The true Photius, alleged by my Preliminary Dissertator to be the *fons et origo* of the tribe of Reviewers, belonged to the ninth century of our era; and his life, even when epitomized, presents the most varied features. Photius was not only a Judge, an Ambassador and a Soldier, but also an Ecclesiastic who in less than a week proceeded Monk, Sub-deacon, Deacon, and Presbyter, ending up on Christmas Day 858 as Patriarch of Constantinople, thus earning for himself the designation of 'All-Holyness'. But though his ecclesiastical rise was rapid beyond precedent, his subsequent fortune was insecure and troubled. The Pope of Rome, though it was no business of his, thought fit to support the claims of the deposed predecessor, and exceeded the papal jurisdiction so far as to excommunicate and anathematize Photius, a step which for the time at all events added to the new Patriarch's popularity as the Champion of Eastern Orthodoxy. After a while Photius was deposed by the Emperor Basil and was indeed lucky to escape assassination by that ruffian. He was, however, restored to the Patriarchate, but only to be again deposed by another Emperor who wanted the post for a relative. Photius died in an Armenian monastery A.D. 891, but only the other day I read in *The Times* that a new Patriarch of Constantinople had been appointed, who on his elevation had, after the passage of more than a thousand years, taken the title of Photius II.

No hopes can be held out to the Reviewers of to-day of such preferment in either Church or State. As a class Reviewers, 'properly so called', are seldom the recipients of honours. Nor am I sorry this should be so, feeling certain that the worst of the batch would be selected for decoration by the ill-informed guardians of the Fountain from whence these blessings flow.

To return to Photius the first. His claim to the paternity of Reviewers will not bear investigation; though its consideration may aid me in my task in determining the Province of the Reviewer.

Photius was almost everything else in the world except a Reviewer.

He was a great Book Collector—which no Reviewer 'properly so called' ever is. The habit of getting books they do not particularly want, for nothing, destroys the palates of Reviewers, whose libraries are usually woeful things to inspect.

Photius was also a great reader of everything that came in his way, and was in the habit of making 'Selections' from the manuscripts he collected, copying out the very words of the authors, thus allowing them to explain themselves in their own way. This is not the general practice of Reviewers.

Photius is no doubt the author of a Compilation entitled *Myriobiblon* or *Bibliotheca*; but this work is reported to me, for I admit it does not lie by my side as I write, to contain nothing but selected passages from the Manuscripts he had read during one journey to Persia as an Ambassador. How this reminds one of Macaulay's journey to India, and of the books he devoured *en route*!

All I can discover about Photius convinces me that though a diligent reader, and a careful recorder of notable passages in the books he read, he was not a 'Reviewer' as we now understand the word.

This method of noting the contents of books without affecting to pass a critical judgment upon them endured for centuries. Our own *Retrospective Review* in 16 volumes (1820–1828) is an excellent example.

The Composers of Manuscripts could not grumble at this method, for as the Copyright of Authors is a modern invention, no writer could complain of his work being epitomized by an Ambassador or anyone else.

The Age of Manuscripts differs from the Age of Print in many ways, but it would be a vulgar error to suppose that even in what are foolishly called the 'Dark Ages', and long before the invention of the movable types, there were not 'Best Sellers' among the Authors whose works were poured forth in thousands from the *Scriptoria* attached to monasteries, and other places. And what is more, the prices obtained for some of these manuscripts would stagger even Dr. Rosenbach.

It may be that St. Gregory and St. Augustine, and their heirs or assigns, were not paid so much a copy for their *Morals* or *City of God*, but had they been, their royalties would have compared with those of Mr. Edgar Wallace, or even with those of the charming young lady who wrote *Gentlemen Prefer Blondes*.

Photius having failed me, I cannot lay my hands upon anyone else at whose door I can lay this screaming brat, anxious as I am to get rid of him.

The Age of Manuscripts was a busy one, even commercially considered; and there certainly were living in the 'Dark Ages' quick-witted men, ready with their pens, satirical rogues, possessed of most of the gifts that play a part in the intellectual outfit of a Reviewer, who had they been wanted by the Trade could have written reviews which would have been, *caeteris paribus*, as good as any appearing after the invention of printing.

But there was no room in those days for the kind of writing we are dealing with; and I do not think it would be safe to look higher for the parentage of a 'Reviewer', 'properly so called', than the Age of Newspapers—using that word in its widest sense.

If this be true, it is probable that the true Parent of the Reviewer as he is known to us is to be found, where we might expect to find him, in France, but no farther back than the middle of the eighteenth century—when Denis de Sallo, a man of position and mark, established in 1755 the *Journal des Savants*, or *Scavans*, as the word was first printed. This was a weekly publication, and contained reviews 'of the most popular and distinguished publications in every department of literature'. The style of this periodical soon became so lively and sarcastic that De Sallo, wishing to shield himself from the blind fury of the Celtic author, published it in the name of his footman, one De Houdonville; thus forestalling by a century Thackeray's Mr. James de la Pluche.

The success of this journal was very great, and attracted to its columns many accomplished writers, whose contributions travelled over Europe, being translated into divers foreign languages, a compliment which has seldom been paid to our native products of criticism.

But though De Sallo and his footman attracted more notice on the Continent, England in point of date was first in the field, for there has never been a publication so unmistakably British as the *Monthly Review*, established in 1749 by Mr. Griffiths and his wife, whose hard bargain with Oliver Goldsmith, perhaps the greatest miscellaneous writer we have ever had, is the subject-matter of some of the best-known anecdotes in the annals of Grub Street.

The *Monthly Review* continued, under different managements, until 1845, and fills 249 volumes. It soon had a rival in Dr. Smollett's *Critical Review*, and on the respective merits of these two Dr. Johnson once expatiated as follows, employing language not wholly irrelevant to our own times:—

'The Monthly Reviewers are not Deists, but they are Christians with as little Christianity as may be, and are for pulling down all establishments. The Critical Reviewers are for supporting the Constitution, both in Church and State. The Critical Reviewers, I believe, often review without reading the books all through, but lay hold of a topick and write chiefly from their own minds. The Monthly Reviewers are duller fellows and are glad to read the books through.'

This last distinction between two classes of Reviewers, those who review without reading, and the duller fellows who for want of any other occupation are glad to read through the books they are called upon to review, is by no means a distinction without a difference. The difference is great, and one that never fails to be noticed by the Authors of the books, who may often be heard complaining first of the Reviewers who do not read the books but write out of their own heads, and secondly of those who do read the books but are too dull to understand them.

The *Monthly* and *Critical Reviews* were considerable undertakings and deserve to be spoken of with a modicum of respect, but their Editors were not on good terms with one another.

In those days Editors were, or appeared to be, differently constituted from the Editor of to-day. There must always be the same sort of rivalry between Editors as between party politicians, but in the Eighteenth Century, whilst rival Editors fought one another in the ring of their rival sheets, to-day they seldom condescend to recognize the existence of any organ of public opinion save 'this Journal', meaning thereby their own trumpet, penny, twopenny, or sixpenny.

Thus we find the rival Editors of the *Monthly* and *Critical* speaking out about each other and their respective staffs with the pleasant freedom of their century. Mr. Griffiths did not hesitate to say, and print, 'that the *Monthly Review* was *not* written by physicians without practice, authors without learning, gentlemen without manners, and critics without judgment', to which the 'Physician without practice', the Author of *Humphrey Clinker* and *Roderick Random*, replied with courage and conviction: 'The *Critical Review* is *not* written by a parcel of hirelings under the restraint of a bookseller and his wife who presume to revise, alter, and amend the articles. Our writers are unconnected with booksellers, unawed by old women, and independent of each other.'

This is an old-fashioned style of writing one ought perhaps to blame, but some of the caps still fit, though to put them on would be bad taste.

It is with reluctance, forced on by the tyranny of my title, that I leave the still glowing ashes of the last century but one, and ask how is the Province of a Reviewer to be determined to-day, and by what Code or *Corpus*—by what Rules or Principles—is his conduct to be guided and controlled?

First of all, how is the business carried on to-day in London, Manchester, Edinburgh and other centres of Civilization? The answer must be that so far as the business consists of reviewing new publications as they appear, it is carried on between the Publishers and the Editors of those newspapers who devote a certain proportion of their columns to new books. This proportion varies from a very small to a considerable one. In the daily papers it is usually small, but in the weekly papers it is sometimes large.

The Publishers' part is to supply the books to the Editors—and it is the part of the Editor to parcel them out among his or her critical hounds.

There is (naturally enough) another column of the newspaper to be taken into account, the Advertisement Column.

Publishers find it necessary to advertise their publications, and wish to do so in those newspapers that enjoy a circulation among the people who are most likely to buy the kind of book that is advertised. A new book on 'the Canon of Scripture' is not advertised in the *Sporting Times*, or a new edition of *Jarman on Wills* in the *Field*.

Editors, therefore, on the lookout for Publishers' and other advertisements, seek to establish for their paper a reputation of one kind or another, literary, religious, scientific, sporting, etc., so as to attract advertisements—either of books or of other wares—from the producers of goods likely to take with the Editors' Public.

This business between the Publishers and Editors is carried on after a 'Give and Take' fashion easier understood than explained in detail —the Publishers supply the Books, and sometimes order the Advertisements, and the Editors do their best to review the Books and send copies of the Reviews to the Publishers.

It is plain that *all* the books and reprints that are received by any well-established Journal with a critical reputation cannot be even so much as noticed, save in the Advertisement Columns, where room somehow or another can usually be found for them.

The output of new publications can only be compared to a huge tidal wave daily or weekly breaking upon an Editor's Table. How is he or she to deal with the wave? Which books are to be reviewed, and how? After the Photian explanatory manner? In the sarcastic style of the *Journal des Savants*? In the vigorous style of the *Monthly* and *Critical Reviews*, or in the now old-fashioned big 'bow-wow' style of the *Edinburgh*[1] and *Quarterly*? and if in the last-named style, how can

[1] Now no more!

room be found in a daily, weekly, or even monthly publication for more than three Reviews at a time?

Never was a day when these questions were so hard to answer. Short notices are just now in great favour with editors, and who can wonder? but neither justice nor injustice can be awarded to good books or bad ones in 1,000 words. The thing cannot be done! Half a dozen poets squeezed into one column! A dozen novels in a column and a half! The publishers may be satisfied, but not the author or the reader of the notice. There is no fun even in Folly unless it is drawn at full length.

When Lord Jeffrey thought fit to make fun of Wordsworth, he did so, being the honest man he was, at great length; with the result that one of his reviews remains to this day the best anthology of Wordsworth yet published; the fact that the Reviewer made his selection from some of the noblest and most heart-stirring lines in English poetry on the ground of their supposed badness and childish absurdity, has been rendered innocuous by the mere lapse of time.

We have only to read the publishing lists of the Oxford and Cambridge Presses, which often, adopting the Photian method, give long extracts from the works enumerated, and those of Messrs. Longmans, Macmillan, Murray, etc., etc., and also keep a watchful eye upon the Biographies,

REVIEWER DETERMINED

Histories, and Academical Theses now wafted across the Atlantic to our shores, to perceive with what an avalanche of print the present-day Reviewer is confronted in all departments of Literature and Science. Why *Sacra Theologia* herself, like a bird escaping from the net of the fowler, is fast repairing her ancient nests in the dim corners of the library.

How are these books to be selected and judged? Some young and lusty Reviewers, so I have been told, are in the habit of descending upon the editorial parlours and carrying off with them to their suburban lairs the review-copies they either wish to add to their own libraries, or because for some reason they deem themselves to be the best qualified to handle the authors' theme. This is a haphazard method of natural selection, and gives an unfair advantage to the able-bodied. The editor should prepare, and keep secret, a list of his Reviewers, recording briefly the nature of their gifts, the extent, so far as he can give a guess, of their learning, and on what subjects they should be forbidden to discourse.

So far, we have been concerned with the business or machinery of reviewing, and now know that the books to be reviewed are sent for nothing by the Publishers to such Editors as they think best. The next step is for the Editor or Sub-Editor or Literary Editor to distribute those of the books he thinks most fitted for the paper among his lions, old or young.

The Lion, young or old, takes the volume or volumes to his own den, and sits down to read for the purpose of discharging the task he owes to his employers and to the reading public.

Lord Morley, on occasions, was fond of talking about old days when he was a Reviewer on the Regular Staff of the *Saturday Review*. It was then his habit once a week to visit the Office, and take home with him the books allotted to him, and in their choice he doubtless had a word to say. In the Office he occasionally encountered other members of the staff who had looked in for the same purpose and were inspecting the provender the publishers had provided.

On these occasions Morley met more than once Lord Robert Cecil, afterwards Lord Salisbury, but they never interchanged words. Why should they? Reviewers are often silent men.

On one of these occasions Morley took home three books: a Cookery Book, a rendering into English of the poems of Catullus, by, I think, Sir Theodore Martin, and a treatise on 'The Operations of War—explained and illustrated' by Sir Edward Hamley.

The Cookery Book and the English Version of Catullus were handled and dispatched *con amore*, but Sir Edward Hamley was returned to the

REVIEWER DETERMINED

Office, and fell to the lot of some other and more warlike member of the staff. This showed at least the glimmering of that Conscience—often denied to Reviewers, particularly and most unjustly to Saturday Reviewers.[1]

We have now got so far on our way of determining the province of a Reviewer as to trace him home bearing his books with him and to leave him pondering his job.

Is he, it will be asked, competent to pass an honest judgment upon the books allotted to him? The answer must depend upon the nature of the book. A young lady, fresh from Miss Pinkerton's Academy or even from the groves of Girton, is obviously not competent to write about Mr. Fearne's *Essay on the Learning of Contingent Remainders and Executory Devises*, even were there any chance of that masterly performance (considered by some the best law book ever written) being reprinted in an Age that is well content to remain in ignorance of the learning of its forerunners.

But speaking more generally, what does Competency mean? Lord Acton, so it is reported, used to read any new historical work, not so much on the chance of its adding anything to his already

---

[1] As an example of excellent reviews or rather essays on general subjects see 'Essays by a Barrister' (the late Mr. Justice Stephen, 1862)—all from the *Saturday Review*.

acquired stock of information (which he thought hardly likely), but to discover how much or how little the Author of the book knew about his subject. It does not follow that Lord Acton's review would have been a better review than the one written by a more ignorant man. It is not so much a question of relative competency as of honesty of purpose. If the Reviewer is careful to confine himself to those aspects of the book on which he feels justified in expressing an opinion, and eschews as an atrocious crime the guilt of attributing to himself the knowledge he has only derived from reading the book, he will seldom have any need to blame himself for undertaking a job beyond his capacity.

The Youthful Reviewer should not often have on his lips the saying 'An ounce of Mother Wit is worth a pound of clergy', but may be permitted to remember that even a learned man may be benefited by the criticisms of a quicker wit.

Honesty is the first thing to lay hold of, and though Honesty requires many things, they need not be dwelt upon, for every man (and even a Reviewer is a man) knows perfectly well when he has ceased to be honest, just as every Plagiarist knows when he is stealing from the work of another. If a Theft is unconscious, it ceases to deserve so harsh a name, but most Plagiarists have been conscious Thieves, and knew perfectly well when they were stealing. And so it is with the dishonest Reviewer.

Reviewers have often been accused by angry Authors of Ignorance and Insolence. Nor can the charge be met with a flat denial. Ignorance and Insolence hunt in couples. But a distinction must be taken, so far as Ignorance is concerned, between Ignorance in matters of Taste, as, for example, of Poetry, and Ignorance in matters of Knowledge. Insolence is always disgusting.

Examples of both kinds of Ignorance may be found in the *Edinburgh Review*. When Lord Jeffrey wrote one of his articles on Wordsworth's poetry in 1807 (see the *E.R.*, vol. xi, p. 214), in which he selects for reprobation and ridicule lines now admitted to be of supreme excellence, he was guilty of bad taste, and the whole article should be read by young Reviewers, if only to show to what lengths of absurdity even a man so intelligent as Lord Jeffrey can be forced to go, when he believes himself possessed of Judicial authority in matters of Taste and Feeling, and finds himself in a position to publish his judgments *orbi et urbi*. If he could have kept his opinions to himself and his clique in Edinburgh, no harm would have been done to his reputation. His folly would have perished with him, but as it is, he swings gibbeted for many a long day, because he thought himself qualified as an arbiter of taste to ridicule a man whose poetical boot-laces he was not worthy to untie.

But Jeffrey's error was an error of taste and judgment, though the insolence of his language was unpardonable.

Ignorance and Insolence both combined in matters of knowledge are to be found in the columns of the same Review, the offender here being that impudent Sciolist, Lord Brougham, and the victim Thomas Young (1775–1829), whose three Memoirs on 'The Theory of Light and Colours' were greedily claimed by Brougham as a subject fit for his hand, and who fell upon them in Nos. 2 and 9 of the *Edinburgh Review*. Young replied, but the harm was done, and the principle that Young had discovered and explained was fourteen years afterwards rediscovered by Fresnel. (See *D.N.B.*, vol. 63, *sub nomine* Young, 393.)

I hope, though I do not know, that Science can now take care of herself, and that the incursions of a Brougham would be repelled with scorn, but what about the sins of Lord Jeffrey? How can a Literary Editor and his staff avoid in the realms of Taste and Feeling the stupid blunders of the Editors of the *Edinburgh* and *Quarterly Reviews*? Can it be done by a judicious snubbing of the bald-headed members of the staff, and bidding them 'stand down', as miners of sixty-

REVIEWER DETERMINED

five are to be bidden no longer to descend the coal-pits, in order to make room for their juniors? This *may* be a prudent method, but if so it must be adopted cautiously, for the Young Men of the present generation become themselves 'back numbers' with amazing celerity.

Are there then no Rules of Criticism to be learnt and applied, and if there are, how are Reviewers to learn to apply them?

Not, we may be sure, as a boy may be taught carpentry at a carpenter's bench, or the art of shaving by practising on sick paupers in a workhouse.

What is called Antiquity has supplied us with authoritative works on the Art of Criticism. To name them would be an affectation of Learning. No one can read them without profit, or without amazement that works so widely read and so greatly admired have still left the province I am dealing with undetermined.

Great Critics have been amongst us, even in modern times, but they have founded no Schools, German, French, or English. To name these Critics would be useless, for to imitate them would be absurd.

How can anyone deliberately set himself to acquire this man's reading or that man's insight?

I must now, being in difficulties, seek shelter

under Authority, and will name, in one breath, Longinus and Gibbon.

The Author of the *Decline and Fall*, after reading the ninth chapter of Longinus, makes the following observations (see Gibbon's *Miscellaneous Works*, vol. v, p. 263):—

'The ninth chapter, which treats of the elevation of ideas, is one of the finest monuments of antiquity. Till now, I was acquainted only with two ways of criticizing a beautiful passage, the one to show, by an exact anatomy of it, the distinct beauties of it, and whence they sprung—the other, an idle exclamatory or a general encomium, which leaves nothing behind it. Longinus has shown me there is a third. He tells me his own feelings upon reading it, and tells them with such energy that he communicates them.'

Here at all events, on the authority of one of the greatest names in English Literature, are three methods of criticizing a work of Taste. The first is by anatomizing its parts in order to exhibit its distinct beauties; the second is an exclamatory O! a gasp of delight, and the third is for the Reviewer to express his own feelings with such energy as to communicate them to his readers.

As for the second of these methods, the exclamatory O! the Reviewer who usually adopts it can hardly be expected to be paid for his labour, though his O was as round as Giotto's; but the other two methods remain open to him, and are, we presume, capable of application to Ugly as well as to Beautiful passages.

To be able to point out the differences between the Sublime and the Ridiculous, the Grand and the Grandiose, between Subtlety and Pretension, between genuine Humour and wire-drawn fancies, between real and false wit, would indeed be a splendid equipment for a Critic, though he would find it difficult to make these distinctions plain to many of his readers.

Fortunately the ordinary Reviewer of ordinary books is not often called upon to draw these fine distinctions and incur enmity by doing so, yet, neither man nor woman can ever write a review worth reading unless they can draw them when necessary.

After Longinus and Mr. Gibbon it may seem a descent to Anthony Trollope, yet writing in 1929 about reviewing books, I could hardly expect to find a more sensible authority, so I will bring these desultory and inconclusive observations to at least one sort of a conclusion by quoting what Trollope has written about a certain Mrs. Brumby.

'We may as well say at once that though Mrs. Brumby might have made a very good Prime Minister, she could not write a paper for a magazine, or produce literary work of any description that was worth paper and ink. We feel sure we may declare without hesitation *that no perseverance on her part, no labour however unswerving, no training however long*, would have enabled her to do in a fitting manner even a review for the *Literary Curricle*.' (See *An Editor's Tales*, Mrs. Brumby.)

These are harsh words to fall from the pen of the most easygoing, the most productive, and the most permanently enjoyable of the Novelists of the Victorian Era, the creator of "Planty Pall", that much-tried husband of the Duchess of Omnium: but the words should be taken to heart by both would-be Reviewers and Editors. No Brumby should be allowed admission.

The habitual Reviewer of new books and reprints is not very likely to be endowed with genius; but if he is an honest workman who loves justice, and eschews malice, and has added a dash of humility in his constitution, and possesses, by grace of Heaven, a drop of that precious Acid enabling him to discern by the ring of the coin whether it comes from the Royal Mint or from a den in the East End, he may, after a while, earn a right to be considered a Reviewer 'properly so called'.

NOTE.—It would be difficult to say when the word *review* as applied to a critical notice of a book as distinguished from an explanatory account of its contents first came into use. Probably about the middle of the Eighteenth Century. Sir John Hawkins, in his now superseded biography of Johnson, has something to say on this subject.

IV

THE BIOGRAPHER OF SIR WALTER SCOTT

IV

THE BIOGRAPHER OF SIR WALTER SCOTT

JOHN GIBSON LOCKHART, 1794-1854

Peter's Letters to his Kinsfolk, 3 vols.	1819
Valerius, 3 vols.	1821
Some Passages in the Life of Adam Blair	1822
Reginald Dalton, 3 vols.	1823
History of Matthew Wald	1824
Ancient Spanish Ballads	1823
The Life of Robert Burns	1828
The Life of Sir Walter Scott, 1st Ed., 7 vols.	1837-38
Lockhart's Life, by Andrew Lang, 2 vols.	1897

IT does not often happen that the name of an accomplished and fecund man of letters becomes exclusively associated with the best of his books. By itself this is not perhaps a misfortune. It may, I think, be said that this is the fate of the Biographer of Scott; and if it is his fate, it is in his case an enviable one.

Bunyan's name is very closely and almost exclusively associated in the public mind with the *Pilgrim's Progress*; so much so that he is as often called the 'Immortal Dreamer' as is Dr. Johnson the 'Great Lexicographer'; but the *Holy War*, the *Life and Death of Mr. Badman*, and *Grace Abounding*, that most precious of autobiographies, are still picked out in the memories of many from the other three hundred works of the man of Bedford —just as *Rasselas* and the *Lives of the Poets* must always crown the labours of the author of the *Dictionary*.

As appears from the incomplete list of books at the head of this article, the Biographer of Scott wrote much besides the great Life of his beloved father-in-law. For instance, he wrote, and published, four novels. To say that no living person has read all these novels would be, so long as Mr. Saintsbury lives—and long may he continue both to live and to work—an obvious untruth. But who else has done so? I would fain add my own name, though it would count for little, but for the fact that with the exception of the *Adam Blair*, for which I have a great regard, I have stuck hopelessly in the remaining three.

Lockhart's four novels never had any success, though he got a much needed £1,000 for one of them. Even the report spread by his enemies, of whom he always had far too many, that his father-in-law wrote them, availed nothing to interfere with their alacrity in sinking.

The 'Younger D'Israeli', as Benjamin (afterwards Earl of Beaconsfield) used to be called in the early thirties, once referred to Lockhart as a tenth-rate novelist, and although it is true that

THE BIOGRAPHER OF SIR WALTER SCOTT

Disraeli disliked Lockhart and though it is also true that Lockhart disliked Disraeli (a dislike shared by many of the latter's contemporaries, including the fourteenth Earl of Derby and the late Marquis of Salisbury), still it cannot be disputed that *Coningsby* is most happily alive, whilst *Reginald Dalton* is, I fear, dead and buried.

It is not therefore as a novelist, or essayist, or critic, or satirist, or poet that Lockhart still holds his own. It is as a great biographer that he occupies his position, not, indeed, the position of first, for Boswell has surpassed him, but one that has never been seriously challenged for the second place.

Lockhart died in 1854, having been pursued with domestic and other sorrows, far surpassing in grief and horror those he has so tenderly and movingly described in his Life of his great relative, and until 1897, when by the happiest of coincidences his own Life came to be written by Andrew Lang, very little was said, written or thought about him, save as Scott's biographer. That most spiteful of journalistic professional obituarists, Miss Martineau, immediately after Lockhart's death, poured a mixed chalice of vitriol and lies over his open grave—but apart from that, after a stormy life, Lockhart's name was left alone in peaceful silence.

I cannot suppose that Mr. Lang's *Life of Lockhart* has had a large sale. The tastes and habits of our reading public are inscrutable, and it may be that the book was just a little bit longer than was necessary; yet the same complaint was made concerning Lockhart's seven volumes about Scott, a complaint which may still be heard repeated in divers dull quarters. Yet just as Lockhart was the one man best qualified of all others to write the Life of Scott at length, so Lang, a Scot, and a Scot of the Border, though separated from his subject by more than forty years, was the very man to describe Lockhart, even as Lockhart had described Sir Walter, tenderly, lovingly, yet firmly and free from all those irritating affectations so prone to disfigure and falsify the work of most biographers.

To laugh and weep over Lockhart's *Life of Scott* you must love Scott, both the man and his books; and to enjoy Lang's *Life of Lockhart* you must also love Scott, for Lockhart was, as it were, Scott's *penumbra*, and the two men, as unlike one another as it is possible for two men of character to be, are for ever bound together in the holy bonds of literature.

Lockhart may have enjoyed little bits of his life, but, as a whole, he had to endure it, from the beginning to the end. After a school and early University education in Glasgow, where his father (who survived him) was (somewhat to Mr. Lang's annoyance) a Presbyterian Divine, Lock-

THE BIOGRAPHER OF SIR WALTER SCOTT

hart proceeded, a boy of fifteen 'in a round jacket', to Balliol College, with a Snell exhibition, and in that seminary became a good classical scholar (of the humane species), and a great student of languages, modern as well as ancient. Before his twentieth year he had taken a First Class and run into debt. In those days (how unlike our own!) no Scot at Balliol need look for a fellowship, and accordingly he had to leave Oxford, carrying back, first to Glasgow and then to Edinburgh, a very considerable store of reading, a face as handsome as Lord Byron's, a quizzical temper, and an unfortunate tendency to caricature his fellow-creatures both with his pen and his pencil.

Thus equipped, he threw himself into the society of a Whig-controlled Edinburgh, a small city, but swarming with Authors and seething with party passion and literary prejudices. He became an Edinburgh Advocate, a profession for the active practice of which he was unfitted. Everyone around him (so at least it seemed to him) was, or was about to become, an Author, and so he became one too.

Mr. Lang thinks that had the youthful Lockhart eschewed Edinburgh and come straight to London he would have found in wider horizons better food for his brain and less acrimonious matter for his spleen.

John Wilson, Macaulay's 'cock-fighting Professor of Moral Philosophy', ten years Lockhart's senior, became his friend, and a worse friend for a young fellow of Lockhart's temperament could hardly have been found. It is only fair to add that the Professor's daughter thought that young Lockhart fostered her Papa's worst faults. It was in any case an unhappy alliance which led to much trouble, mischief, and enduring sorrow for Lockhart.

Lockhart unfortunately did not make Scott's acquaintance at once, but when he did it ripened quickly, and from the first Scott looked upon Lockhart almost as a son, though he kept back from him the nature of his secret business relations with the Ballantyne Brothers, knowing well how repulsive they would be to the haughty Hidalgo who had become his son-in-law.

To tell the story of Lockhart's life and sorrows, even in brief, would be to impose too great a strain upon the reader, and I will therefore be content to advise all lovers of Scott, and good literature, and Andrew Lang, to read for themselves, at their leisure, if they ever have any, the *Life of Lockhart* by his brother Borderer.

One word must be added. Lockhart was Editor of the *Quarterly Review* from October 1825 to July 1853. He was not well fitted for the post. An 'Hidalgo', with a scornful countenance, an indifferent manner, and a well-cultivated contempt for his fellow-creatures, whether publishers, contributors, or readers, could hardly be a good Editor, even of a quarterly magazine.

His was a hard fate, and it is beautiful to notice how keen is Andrew Lang's sympathy for the Editorial Lockhart. When the latter took over Mr. Murray's Review, that best and most unbearable of men, Robert Southey, was its oldest, most regular, best paid, and longest-winded contributor. Lockhart never took to Southey, and cut him down as much as he was permitted to do—for in those days Southey had a great reputation. Next in order of importance was the egregious Croker, with what Lockhart calls his 'beloved religion', a compound which in Croker's stomach was at once turned into something it would be an insult to the whole tribe of 'Mammalia' to call even 'sour milk'. (Read Croker's notes to Lord Hervey's *Memoirs* and to the *Letters* of Lady Hervey, and you will grasp the full significance of Lockhart's reference.) Then there was the effete but still productive Sir John Barrow, and young Mr. Gladstone, never effete, but always both productive and dangerous.

Lockhart found his most trusted contributor in the Rev. H. H. Milman, then regarded as a pious Byron. Nobody who reads Lang's account of Lockhart's life will ever wish to be an Editor.

THE BIOGRAPHER OF SIR WALTER SCOTT

Towards the end of Lockhart's life he became acquainted with Carlyle and the two men took at once to one another, with an almost brotherly affection. It was a pity they seldom met, but Lockhart lived in Sussex Place in the Regent's Park, rather out of the reach of Chelsea and a somewhat unknown region to the elder man. In 1842 Lockhart sent some verses of his own to Carlyle, which, clinging as they did to the ever-tenacious memory of their recipient, were often repeated by him in the solitary and stricken old age that was to lie before him.

> 'It is an old belief
> That on some solemn shore
> Beyond the sphere of grief
> Dear friends shall meet once more.
>
> 'Beyond the sphere of Time
> And Sin and Fate's control,
> Serene in changeless Prime
> Of Body and of Soul.
>
> 'That creed I fain would keep,
> This hope I'll not forgo—
> Eternal be the sleep,
> Unless to waken so.'

A moving cry of the heart—but hardly a Christian cry. It is not for mortals to dictate to the Almighty the company they insist on meeting in Heaven.

V

JOHN WYCLIF

V

JOHN WYCLIF

THERE are not two more resounding names in English ecclesiastical history than those of John Wyclif and John Wesley. Separated as they are from one another by 'whole centuries of folly, noise, and sin', and unlike one another in nearly all respects save in their common manhood and determination to do their own thinking in their own way, they are alike in this, they were both devoted sons of the University of Oxford.

Dr. Workman, who we cannot help suspecting is in the same plight himself, has managed to find room in his closely woven and almost too crowded pages for the following outburst from the pen of Wyclif, written at the end of his days:—

'Not unworthily is it called the vineyard of the Lord. It was founded by the holy fathers, and situated in a splendid site, watered by rills and fountains—surrounded by meadows, pastures, plains, and glades; the mountains and hills around it ward off the spirit of the storm, while it is near to flourishing groves and leafy villages. I will sum up all in one word. Oxford is a place gladsome and fertile, so suitable for the habitation of the gods that it has been rightly called the House of God and the Gate of Heaven.'

JOHN WYCLIF

We are glad to quote, at the outset (though without prejudice) this rapturous passage (translated from the Latin), for it glows with a personal fervour and note of affection seldom noticeable in Wyclif's writings.

Apart from a common love for Oxford, a love that has lingered through the centuries, and links Wyclif with Newman, all resemblances between the two resounding names of Wyclif and Wesley soon vanish. Between 1324 and 1703, their reputed birth-years, there is a gulf only to be bridged by outstanding traits of a common humanity, and, unfortunately, the earlier John has left behind him few such traces on the sand. Wyclif's books are for the ordinary reader (save for some passages in his native tongue) frankly unreadable; and his life, so far as it can be made known to us, is always puzzling—often unedifying, and very seldom inspiring.

Dr. Workman is far too true and long-suffering a scholar to grow angry with his subject, for whom he has a great admiration, but at times even from him a sympathetic reader seems to overhear a stifled groan, shall we say? over the 'impersonality' of his great man, and the almost entire absence of those 'human touches' so dear to the picturesque biographer, and indeed essential to the making of a biography as distinct from a treatise or a history. A Huss or a Tyndale would

JOHN WYCLIF

have been a pleasanter job. But honest biographers must take their men and materials as they are provided. Novelists and propagandists may do what they like.

Nor is it easy to trace the development of this arch-heretic's mind from decade to decade. Wyclif's Oxford Tracts travelled far and wide even in his day of manuscripts and of the most amazing clerical illiteracy; and wherever they went they proved themselves to be Tracts *for* and not *against* the times, but *this* tractarian has left no *Apologia pro sua vita* behind him.

Yet it must have come about somehow—this gradual change from Catholic orthodoxy to open revolt with organized Christianity as then existent. It seems to have begun with Church politics and abuses and to have ended with Church doctrines. If the Popes of Rome could have been content either to abandon altogether or quickly to let drop their right of reservation of bishoprics and livings in England, Wyclif might have held his tongue a little longer, but Italian cardinals, and 'olive-faced padres from Spain', whether resident, or, like himself, non-resident in English archdeaconries and parishes, were too much for his Yorkshire blood, and he began letting himself go.

Dr. Workman deals faithfully with his readers, and by the time the second of his two volumes is laid down has administered such a dose of the 'medieval mind' that the reader in question can hardly fail to come up gasping for breath; unless, indeed, his previous perusal of such fascinating books as Dr. A. I. Carlyle's *Medieval Theory in the West* and Mr. Poole's *Illustrations of the History of Medieval Thought and Learning* have made him partially acquainted with the difficulties attendant upon delving in those fields.

And to make Dr. Workman's task (most manfully performed) all the harder Wyclif is not an attractive writer in himself.

He was an immense reader and quoter, and quotes St. Augustine almost as often as Montaigne quotes Plutarch, but he never succeeds in catching even a tincture of the dominating charm of either Augustine or Montaigne, whilst his logic is so defective that almost anyone can see the gaps; and thus he never holds you in his grip after the relentless fashion, so hard to escape from, of his successor in heterodoxy and a kindred theologian, the great John Calvin.

Still, Dr. Workman struggles on, and he has his reward in the gratitude of the reader—but no reviewer dare follow him. For example, the earliest and largest of Wyclif's works are his treatises *De dominio divino* and *De civili dominio*. Listen to Dr. Workman for a moment or two on the latter work:—

JOHN WYCLIF

'In his *De civili dominio* Wyclif further developed his doctrine of lordship. This vast work of over a thousand pages is preserved in a single Vienna manuscript, written probably by a Czech student between 1407 and 1410. In spite of its inordinate length and "digressions, meanderings, excursions innumerable", the treatise has value because of the interest attaching to the two "truths" with which it opens, one that no man in mortal sin can hold *dominium* or lordship; the other that everyone in a state of grace has real lordship over the whole universe.'

These are far-reaching 'truths', and the first of them is never likely to be accepted by, say, the millionaire proprietors of our syndicated Press, no one of whom would have the hardihood to swear in a court of law that he was ever in a state of grace.

We can pursue this subject no farther, but in fairness to Wyclif it should be stated that his 'two truths' are firmly based on notions of feudality, then prevalent in Europe. Wyclif held that God's government was a feudal government, but without mesne lords, or, as Mr. Poole puts it, 'all men held directly of God, with differences in accidentals, but in the main fact of their tenure all alike'.

Feudality has perished in fact long ago, and we live now in an age of weekly wages determined by the 'two truths'—the right of the workmen to strike, and the right of the masters to lock out, whilst between these millstones, the upper and the lower, the consumer plays the part of the grain and is ground accordingly.

Another of Wyclif's statements in his *De civili dominio* is the right of the State over the property of the Church, and he takes occasion in his treatise *De Veritate Scripturae*,

'to reaffirm his convictions that only by disendowment, especially the withholding of tithes from bad priests, can the interests of the realm be adequately guarded, the spread of the gospel be secured, the Church be purified, and the intentions of pious founders be fulfilled, and as a corollary "he defends the right of laymen to pass judgment on Priests".'

But for the blessed truth that there was no Holy Inquisition in England, and that the law *de heretico comburendo* did not make its appearance on the Statute-book until 1401, some fifteen years after Wyclif's natural death in his rectory at Lutterworth, we should almost hear the crackling of the faggots in these words.

Wyclif proceeded fast from heresy to heresy, until in his *De potestate Papae* he maintained that 'England is not bound to obey the Pope, except so far as obedience can be deduced from Scripture', and in the summer of 1379 at Oxford he pub-

JOHN WYCLIF

lished his first attack on the Roman doctrine of the Eucharist.

We cannot here proceed farther, but before we bid Wyclif a short farewell, something must be said about his translations from the Vulgate of portions of the Old and New Testaments into English, 'as she was spoken' in the fourteenth century.

Dr. Workman's chapter entitled 'Wyclif and the Bible' tells this story candidly, and fully; but if the reader would like to hear more about how many bits of Holy Scripture were in circulation in Middle English before Wyclif's time, he can read about this in Miss Deansley's *Lollard Bible*, and in Cardinal Gasquet's *Old English Bible*. It is, in some of its details, a slightly controversial story, in which Sir Thomas More takes a hand.

Though it is now plain that Wyclif did not, with his own hand, translate the whole Vulgate, or even large parts of it, into English, nothing can rob him of the distinction of having been the first great Bible Christian in England, for truly it can be said of him in his later years that the Bible, and the Bible alone, was the religion of John Wyclif.

Wyclif was, like Wesley, a great preacher, and like Wesley and Spurgeon, he preached the Bible, intermingling his translations from the Vulgate as

JOHN WYCLIF

he went along with his own commentaries upon the text. He knew neither Greek nor Hebrew, but he must have known the Vulgate as well as Dr. Newman knew King James's Version. That he also translated and published certain portions of the Bible, and inspired and assisted other translators, notably John Purvey (who outlived him and laboured in the same work to the end of a harassed life), is certain—and eventually the *Wycliffe Bible* appeared in manuscript, in which condition it was allowed to remain until our own time.

Nothing ought to be said to injure the fame of that learned Biblical Scholar and Martyr unto death, William Tyndale, who was the first translator of the whole Bible into the noble English still familiar to our ears, as we catch its echoes in the Authorized Version.

It may well be that Wyclif's otherwise questionable relationship with John of Gaunt saved him from the harsh treatment that befell some of his fellow-workers at Oxford and elsewhere, and secured for him a natural death.

Wyclif died on December 31st, 1384, three days after hearing Mass in his church at Lutterworth, and as he was not under any formal excommunication, his friends, by whom he was surrounded, were able to bury him according to the Christian rites.

JOHN WYCLIF

More than forty years afterwards this wrong was remedied, for in the spring of 1428, in pursuance of peremptory orders from the Pope, the bones of the old Master of Balliol were dug out of the earth, burnt to ashes, and flung into the little river Swift, 'to the damnation and destruction of his memory'.

But even a Martin V, though carrying out (somewhat tardily) the strict injunctions of an Œcumenical Council, the Council of Constance, that burnt John Huss, cannot control men's minds or dictate their memories. The name of John Wyclif still resounds through his native land; and as for his poor ashes, Fuller's words will always rise to our lips.

We are grateful to Dr. Workman for these fruits of his labours, which cover much more ground than the history of the life and death o Wyclif. It was a hard book to write, and if a slenderly equipped critic may venture to say so, he has done it well.

VI

JOHN BUNYAN

VI

JOHN BUNYAN

LINKS OF EMPIRE (BOOKS)

(The Pilgrim's Progress from this World to that which is to come. Delivered in the Similitude of a Dream. 1678.)

I CONFESS to having been not a little puzzled over the title of this series of articles that seems to connect after some sort of fashion two such separate continents of feeling as are summoned to our thoughts by the utterance of the two words Books and Empire. Both are master-words, exciting memories and fears, thoughts of progress and decay; both are crowned with great names and wonderful exploits; and if their respective histories are not infrequently soiled and even disgraced, it is with the soil of that human nature out of which all men have sprung.

How are such continents to be linked?

Empires are separative things—'Divide and Rule' is an imperial maxim, Universal Empire a bad dream, ending in a nightmare.

Literature, however embarrassed by the Tower

of Babel, however deep embedded in Nationalism and enriched by local and untransferable colours, is world-wide and refuses to be set out by metes and bounds. If it seldom conquers, it can mitigate the antipathies of race, and sailing across estranging seas can pass the barricades of hostile religions, and force men to recognize that the same heart lurks in every human breast.

The conquests of Literature, though they may be few in number and limited in scope, have not, so far as they have yet extended, been accomplished under the flags of Empire, though they may, like trade (a word more usually associated with Empire), have followed it. These literary conquests have been won by 'peaceful penetration', and their arms and ammunition have been supplied, not by the blood and bones of conscripts, nor by the vulpine impulses of commerce, but by the printing-presses of Venice and Parma, of Rome, Paris, and London, and other centres of civilization, which for years past have thrown the literatures of the Western world into hotchpot. A Chauvinist in letters seldom raises his head save during the moments of frenzied war, and long, long before the war has been paid for the Chauvinist is forgotten.

The one drawback to the invention of the movable types is that it circulates human folly and vulgarity as readily as it does wisdom and

JOHN BUNYAN

common sense, and, as the momentary demand for the former commodities is always greater than for the latter, injury to men's mentality is done. But, when we compare the advantages we have gained, and remember the long time it takes to educate even a small planet like this world, we may be thankful the injury is not worse. It does not do to be too squeamish about bad jokes or vulgar journalism or films.

Dismounting, however, from this high horse of argumentation, it may, we think, be said from a pedestrian point of view and as a plain matter of fact that there are books that follow the emigrant —be he British, French, German, Italian, or Spanish—all over the world, and carry with them the sense of home, and in that way may honestly be called 'Links of Empire'.

In Victorian days it used to be said that every English settler in Canada or Australia carried with him into his log cabin two books—the Bible in King James's Version and Macaulay's Essays. This saying was, doubtless, first promulgated in Fleet Street by some stay-at-home journalist who had never travelled two hundred miles from 'The Cock Tavern', and who would have been far too put out by the log cabin's lack of his accustomed nourishment to have derived much solace from either of the two volumes in the settler's small but well-selected library. Still, the saying was inspired, and, allowing for the divine afflatus of the period of George Augustus Sala, had truth behind it.

The fact is, no one can even pretend to estimate the force of good literature over untutored minds. The 'masses' are dumb dogs, and in no way addicted to writing appreciations of their favourite authors. They read very little, and they seldom write at all; but this proves nothing. A man's enjoyment of a book that takes his fancy is not to be measured by the number of books he has read, but by his capacity for enjoyment, and it often happens that the more exclusive his familiarity with one book the greater is his enjoyment of it. Could a list be made of the books that have been most widely read all over the Western world since, say, the fourth century of this era, it would be full of literary instruction, provided it was not made from a conventional point of view.

The big 'bow-wows' of literature, though never really to be over-praised, are made to suffer by a conventional gratitude oftener expressed than felt. The insincere puffing of great authors who are bound to live does more harm than the dishonest puffing of small ones doomed to die.

No books, even in the domicile of their origin, are read everywhere, always, and by all. Who was it who exclaimed, when he discovered a dog's-eared copy of Thomson's *Seasons* on a bench in a country inn, 'This is fame!'? To-day, a thirsty pedestrian, if lucky enough to find the door of a village inn open as he passes, is not likely to find a copy of Thomson's *Seasons* in the bar parlour; and, if he does, unless he has the luck to open it at the pleasing incident of 'Musidora bathing', would he think it worth his notice? Even so admirable a poet as Thomson must be content with a small allotment of anything that can be called 'fame'.

Nevertheless, there are, to employ Charles Lamb's phrase (though I have not the courage to give as he did several examples of his meaning), 'Great Nature's stereotypes of perpetually reproductive volumes', of which it may be said that even at this moment they show no active signs of serious wear and tear—and amongst these *The Pilgrim's Progress* is, perhaps, the best exemplar.

Tried by the log-cabin test, *The Pilgrim's Progress* would emerge triumphant, for, if publishers' and printers' records are to be trusted, there are, at the present moment, more copies of Bunyan's romance or drama or allegory, call it by what name you choose, in existence than of any other English book, excepting King James's Version of the Bible.

Could any book be injuriously affected by praise (and the praise of authors of their predecessors, when dead, is sometimes suspiciously unreal), it would be *The Pilgrim's Progress*, for, ever since it began to be noticed at all by the race of professional critics, it has been, with no exceptions worth mentioning, praised without stint, reserve, or qualification. Pious Christians, whether evangelically minded or, like Coleridge, addicted to philosophy and metaphysics, men of letters untinged by religion like Lord Macaulay, men of business like Benjamin Franklin, lovers of adventure, and slaves to style, have all combined to shower praise on this little book. Even faithful Romanists have allowed their love of literature to prevail over their dread of heresy, and have recognized, as Dr. Newman did, that John Bunyan had some of the notes of a Saint about him. It is true that a few querulous High Churchmen, like the Archidiaconal father of the two Froudes, kept the *Pilgrim* out of the way of their children; a step that did not secure the orthodoxy of his offspring. Speaking generally, Bunyan has, without challenge or demur, taken his place at the high table of English literature, where he composedly holds his own, and far more than his own, though an unordained Baptist preacher, among the Hookers and the Taylors and the other big-wigs of the Establishment.

In point of sheer imaginative genius, as applied to what Coleridge has called the *Summa Theologiae Evangelicae*, Bunyan soars above them all. 'I know of no book,' says S. T. C. (see *Literary Remains*, vol. iii, p. 391), 'the Bible excepted, which I, according to my judgment and experience, could so safely recommend as reaching and enforcing the whole saving truth according to the mind that was in Jesus Christ as *The Pilgrim's Progress*'.

Bunyan has so often been called a tinker that it is hardly worth while to criticize this use of a word that no longer carries with it any imputation. Most modern Prime Ministers have been called tinkers—their pots and pans being Acts of Parliament and election pledges. As a matter of fact, Bunyan was not the kind of tinker who might be called 'a carpet-bagger', that is, one who wanders about the country, pitching his tent in dingles and dells and mending the kettles he often steals, but was a resident brazier of Bedford, paying (when not in prison for preaching 'Christ crucified') scot and lot, like any other citizen. Mr. Dick, we remember, hit upon the profession of a brazier as the most suitable one for David Copperfield. A proof of even mid-Victorian respectability.

Macaulay has called Bunyan 'illiterate', and so he was in the sense that he, like many another author, wrote more than he had read, for, in addition to *The Pilgrim's Progress* and *The Holy War*, his printed publications fill two stout folio volumes.

The village school at Elstow, which Bunyan

as an infant attended, must have been a sound seminary, for there he was taught three things seldom acquired at the Universities, viz., to write legibly, to think clearly, and to speak plainly. No doubt, in after-life, Bunyan is found disparaging his old school, and stating that he forgot all he had been there taught, and had to learn it all over again. But this is a familiar grumble, and Bunyan was always over-disposed to exaggerate both his sins and his disadvantages.

Bunyan was condemned to live in a bad period of English history. Most historical periods are bad, but Bunyan's period (1628–1685) was a very bad one indeed. To what extent, and on which side, Bunyan took part in the tussle between the King and the Parliamentary forces we do not know, for, though Bunyan was an autobiographical man, on these points, as on so many others, he preserved strict silence. That he had carried arms and taken part in a siege, probably of Leicester, is certain, but that is all we can be certain about, except that the author of *The Holy War* was a martially minded man.

Our Civil War was not conducted with savagery. The forces, like the nation, were equally divided. The nobility were divided—and so were the gentry. The Inns of Court leaned to the Parliament, and, as for the peasantry, they, save in certain districts, were well content to take as little of the war as possible. In the few large towns it was different.

It was after the war was over, and the Cromwellian usurpation had come to the end of all military despotisms, and another Charles was misbehaving himself in Whitehall, that Bunyan's real troubles began. By this time religion, and, what is more, the Christian religion, had got hold of him, and he became what his acquaintances called him, a 'walking concordance of the Bible'. A born preacher, with a vocabulary going straight to the heart, he drew large congregations in the open air or in unlicensed conventicles. His imagination had taken fire, and, long ere he had composed a line of his masterpiece, he must have produced and described in a hundred vivid discourses Christian's flight from the Town of Destruction to the eternal City of God.

This was the time when the two worst and most cruel enemies English Nonconformists have ever had, Lord Clarendon and Archbishop Sheldon, were enforcing with horrible brutality, aided by a subservient Cavalier Parliament, that very Act of Uniformity of 1662 which Archbishop Davidson is at this moment attempting to duplicate.[1]

John Bunyan was a Baptist *ex animo*—that is, a believer in men and women publicly declaring

[1] The attempt failed owing to an adverse vote in the House of Commons. (See last Essay.)

themselves Christians in a heathen world when, and not before, they knew what they were about. This was lucky for us, though hard upon him and his innocent children he loved so well, for, had he been content to remain a State Churchman and to attend the ministrations of the Rev. Mr. Two-tongues instead of preaching on his own account, his imagination must have withered, and this particular 'Link of Empire' never have been forged.

He was, as all know, clapped into Bedford Gaol, where he remained off and on for twelve years. He could have got out more than once, but on terms of not preaching, and to this he would never consent. The obstinacy of some men is remarkable. The date of Bunyan's final release was early in 1672.

We are bound to believe that our Link of Empire was forged in Bedford Gaol, because Bunyan tells us it was, though only casually in a marginal note inserted in the second edition of the first part. But, if composed in prison, how are we to explain the fact that it was not published until 1678, years after the author was finally set at liberty? If so composed, it must have been begun at the very end of the captivity, for it bears all the signs of hasty writing, and even then there are left five years or more to explain. Bunyan has given us in rhyme the reasons for this otherwise inexplicable delay. A communicative soul, and not averse to the sound of his own voice, he had read his manuscript to groups of pious friends of the Nonconformist persuasion, and their verdict was far from unanimous.

'Some said, John, print it; others said, Not so.
Some said, It might do good; others said, No.'

It is easy to understand this difference of opinion among the godly. The pious folk of a generation that really believed in the Bible, as then interpreted, instinctively disliked the drama. 'Plays and Puritans' were then, as now, antagonistic, and this was not because a Puritan could see nothing enjoyable in a play, but because he felt that there was in him a far too great capacity for enjoyment. I can hear one of these brethren saying to Bunyan, 'John, this book of yours is so exciting and the life-like adventures of your Christian so spell-binding that young and impressionable souls will read it for pleasure and let the profit go hang!' And so they have, from 1678 till to-day, by millions!

Bunyan may have taken his time before making up his mind, but *The Pilgrim's Progress* was never in any serious danger of being thrown into his brazier's forge. The *Æneid* of Virgil may have run some such risk, for the great Mantuan was a self-conscious artist, and well aware that even the fires of genius may burn low if too assiduously poked. The vanity of an author may usually be relied upon to see that the grate is empty when he flings his manuscript into it.

The manuscript was eventually sent to Mr. Ponder in the Poultry, and in 1678 the first part of *The Pilgrim's Progress* slipped into the world—a tiny, cheap book, printed on yellowish-grey paper. No price is named on the title-page—probably it was eighteenpence. Only four copies of this first edition are now known to be in existence, and for one of these copies (an immaculate one) somebody lately gave £6,800. A large sum to give for an edition of *The Pilgrim's Progress* that does not contain Mr. Worldly Wiseman, in which Giant Despair has no wife, and in which Mr. Facing Both Ways is not mentioned.

These additions were at once made by the author, and appeared in the second and third editions that followed very quickly after the first. The famous 'cuts' appeared in the eighth edition.

I have always thought that the interview between Mr. Worldly Wiseman and Christian, coming as it does at the very beginning of the Allegory, exhibits Bunyan at his highest points of insight and expression. The philosophy of Wiseman and the language in which he clothes it reveals the whole school of Deists and Erastian churchmen of the succeeding century. The passage is too long and too familiar to be quoted.

JOHN BUNYAN

Happily, none of us read *The Pilgrim's Progress* in the first edition! When Worldly Wiseman wonders why Christian should run such desperate risks to obtain he knows not what, Christian replies in piercing words that have reverberated through the world, 'I know what I would obtain—it is ease for my heavy burden'.

The second part appeared in 1684 and is often said to be the best second part that has ever appeared to a work of the highest genius. Nobody is bound to be of this opinion. The second part certainly begins very badly, the dream Christiana has of 'her late espoused saint', harped and crowned, eating and drinking in Heaven in a palatial house of his own, is most un-Bunyan-like and distasteful. As the story advances it improves, and contains some truly glorious passages and amusing by-play. The presence of the gallant Great-Heart, who personally conducts the pilgrims, and chops off the head of Giant Despair, and generally performs feats of amazing valour, takes away from the excitement of the adventure. There are no real 'thrills' in the second part of *The Pilgrim's Progress*.

Had Bunyan lived longer he might have perpetrated a third part, but, dying as he did in 1688, he was, happily as I think, prevented from doing so.

It has been said over and over again, and at

this no one need wonder, for it was Macaulay who first said it, that *The Pilgrim's Progress* 'was perhaps (an unusual word on Macaulay's lips) the only book about which after the lapse of a hundred years the educated minority has come over to the opinion of the common people'. There is substance in this dictum; but, when he says 'that until a recent period all the numerous editions were evidently meant for the "cottage and the servants' hall",' he forgot a costly edition that first appeared in 1728 with illustrations by John Sturt, whose edition of the Book of Common Prayer, 'the frontispiece being a portrait of George the First, in which was inscribed the Creed, the Lord's Prayer, the Prayer for the Royal Family and the Twenty-first Psalm', must have been a treat to handle, whilst his edition of *The Pilgrim's Progress* was almost equally sumptuous—but the children of the hall, like those of the cottage, still went on preferring the villainous 'cuts' of the seventeenth century. Since 1728 it would be hard to say how many artists and engravers have been employed to illustrate John Bunyan. Stothard's plates are, perhaps, the best.

Now comes the last question to be asked, and a teasing, tiresome question it is, belonging to the kind that Bunyan in a terrifying passage refers to as having been suggested to his Pilgrim 'just when he was come over against the mouth of the burning pit', by one of the wicked ones who 'stepped up closely to him and whisperingly suggested to him many grievous blasphemies which he verily thought had proceeded from his own mind'. What, you may well ask, is this blasphemous question? It is this—how many readers, eager, impassioned readers, has *The Pilgrim's Progress* to-day? It was in all the shops at Christmas-tide; it is on our shelves, but is it being firmly lodged in the minds and memories of the rising generations, both here at home and 'by the long wash of Australasian seas'? Poor Madge Wildfire had the book by heart, as we are reminded in a memorable passage in the most moving of all the Waverley Novels, but has by this time the romance lost any of its catching charm? Has the story lost any of its grip? Has the Allegory worn thin? Does the 'link' show signs of giving way to the pressure of doubt? These are questions apt to come 'in the wintry season when the vital sap of faith retires to the root', but they must be faced. I am not of those who think that doubts proceed from the devil and should be crushed on the threshold. Many melancholy examples of the bad effects of this drastic treatment are to be found in what are called 'religious' biographies.

One obstacle that might easily be supposed to lie in the way of Bunyan's continued popularity

JOHN BUNYAN

lies in his theology, which was frankly Calvinistic; and Calvinistic theology as a scheme of divinity is not only out of fashion, but has passed beyond the regions of human belief.

The theology of *The Pilgrim's Progress*, though Calvinistic in hue, is not the black Calvinism of the Rev. Augustus Toplady, the author of that great hymn, 'Rock of Ages'. A strong taint of Arminianism found its way, under the pressure of the story, into *The Pilgrim's Progress*. You have only to read how Christian disposed of Mr. Talkative, who had 'taken in' that nice, dear fellow Faithful, to discover how Bunyan, like Charles Wesley, and unlike Toplady, was disposed to think that 'in the day of doom men shall be judged according to their fruits'.

It is not Bunyan's Calvinism that may strangle his story. The danger, if danger there is, lies elsewhere.

When Bunyan dreamt his dream in Bedford Gaol, and saw Christian emerging out of the Valley of the Shadow of Death and approaching the Cave where once upon a time dwelt two mighty Giants, Pope and Pagan, who had in days gone by wrought great mischief on passing Pilgrims to the Celestial City, he tells us that, when Christian came up to the Cave, there was only one of the two Giants left, for Giant Pagan had long since disappeared, 'dead many a day'. Only Giant Pope was in his old place, and too feeble to frighten even a Mr. Timorous.

To-day it is very different. Giant Pagan has come back again, more powerful than ever. Giant Pope also has somewhat miraculously recovered the use of his limbs, but were Bunyan to come to life again I do not think he would regard the Pope as the real enemy of Christian faith in its integrity. If Paganism prevails it may well be that the popularity of *The Pilgrim's Progress* will suffer an eclipse.

Let me end upon the note of Empire. In the doggerel lines Bunyan prefixed to his second part, he proudly boasts how his Pilgrim had crossed the narrow seas:—

'In France and Flanders, where men kill each other,
My Pilgrim is esteem'd a friend, a brother,
In Holland, too, 'tis said, as I am told,
My Pilgrim is with some worth more than gold.'

Nor did the Pilgrim shirk the broad Atlantic.

' 'Tis in New England under such advance,
Receives there so much loving countenance
As to be trim'd, new cloth'd, and deck'd with gems,
That it may show its features and its limbs.
Yet more, so comely doth my Pilgrim walk
That of him thousands daily sing and talk.'

JOHN BUNYAN

If it be true that *The Pilgrim's Progress* is a 'Link of Empire', no news would be so grateful to John Bunyan, who, more than any of our authors of the very first rank, was a plain Englishman to the core, and as good an Imperialist as it is possible for any Christian to be.

VII

GEORGE WHITEFIELD

VII

GEORGE WHITEFIELD

(An Address delivered to the Whitefield's Men's Mission, Tottenham Court Road, on the occasion of the unveiling of a Bust of George Whitefield. May 1916.)

I AM honoured by having been invited to come this afternoon to unveil the bust of George Whitefield which has been presented to this place, identified with his name, by the generosity of Mr. Passmore Edwards, who has wished me also to associate the name of Mr. Pegram, the sculptor, a proficient in that noble art. At the present moment I am so situated that I cannot derive much inspiration from the bust, except in so far as any inspiration is to be found in an admirable counterfeit of an eighteenth-century wig. Very few words of mine are needed this afternoon. George Whitefield, although he was born in a public-house in Gloucester, and although he did for a time in his early manhood—boyhood, rather—pursue the somewhat unhallowed vocation of a tapster, nevertheless came of a clerical ancestry, for his great-grandfather, his great-great-grandfather, and his great-great-great-grandfather were rectors and vicars of the Established Church. Whitefield suffered, or enjoyed, what is called an irregular education. I do not think it mattered very much with him, for after all, although I fear what I am saying is rank heresy, education is largely controlled by temperament. And Whitefield's temperament was always that of the orator and the actor rather than of the scholar; his concern was with the spoken rather than with the written word. His mother, however, an excellent woman, was concerned with his education, and did her utmost to persuade him to take what he could get in days when there was no national system of either primary or secondary education. She persuaded him to go, as a servitor, to the University of Oxford. In the Eighteenth Century the University of Oxford, though not exactly open to the public, was usually open to poor scholars, provided the would-be entrant either was, or was prepared to become, a communicating member of the Established Church, and had no *prior* objections to Cranmer's Thirty-nine Articles, and was ready to submit to the somewhat servile though in no sense disgraceful conditions appertaining to the lot of the poor scholar. In the Eighteenth Century servitors have risen to become Archbishops of Canterbury, taking rank next to the King. George Whitefield proceeded to Pembroke College as a servitor, some months after the date when another famous man, also poor but by no means humble-minded, Samuel Johnson, had left the same College without a degree, to seek, with David Garrick, his fellow-townsman, their fortunes in the great City—not of Lichfield but of London.

We do not know much of either Johnson's or Whitefield's College life, though the latter has told us that it was one of his duties as a servitor to go round the rooms in College after ten o'clock p.m., and see that their various occupants were inside them, and how in the course of that duty he often met the devil on the staircase. What precise significance he attached to those words I have never been able quite accurately to ascertain. So far as I know—at all events, so far as I remember—it is one of the few remarks he makes about his University life. One other circumstance, however, he does refer to. He says that before he went to Oxford he had just seen Law's *Serious Call to a Devout and Holy Life*, but he had been too poor to buy the book. When, however, he was at Oxford, he saw the book in the hands of a friend, and he obtained possession of it, and in touching language he describes how the Lord wrought wonderfully upon his soul through the agency of that book. And it is rather significant that Dr. Johnson, himself a Christian and an earnest man, though of a different type and calibre than Whitefield, also says that during his University career he took up, in an idle mood, this book of Law's, thinking rather to make fun of it, and it took possession of his soul. How wonderful is the power of a good book!

Before he went to Oxford, Whitefield had become slightly acquainted with those who had just begun to be called Methodists. He had had some communication with Charles Wesley, and when he came up to Oxford he found the Oxford Methodist movement in its beginning. Oxford has always been the home of thought-movements, some in one direction, some in another—movements not to be disregarded, to be spoken lightly of, or to be despised; for men's thoughts, the channels in which men's thoughts run if they are serious and in earnest, never fail to make their influence felt. George Whitefield did not indeed become a Methodist in any formal sense of the word whilst he was at Oxford, but he joined the Society, I believe, very shortly after he left there.

He was ordained a deacon in the Church of England in 1739 by the Bishop of his native town, Bishop Benson, and he was ordained a priest at Christ Church, in Oxford, by the same prelate acting by the permission of Dr. Secker, who was then Bishop of Oxford. This Bishop Benson, it so happened, had been in early life the tutor of Lady Huntingdon with whom Whitefield became so closely connected, and in Lady Huntingdon's *Life* we read rather a curious story. 'On the Countess's adopting the sentiments of the two reformers', that is, Whitefield and Wesley, 'her husband recommended us to converse with the Bishop, and when this request was readily received, the Bishop was accordingly sent for, we suppose, as the Shunammite sent for Elisha, and he attempted to convince her ladyship of the unnecessary strictness of her conduct, but she pressed him so hard with Scripture, and brought so many quotations from the Articles and Homilies, so plainly and faithfully urged upon him the responsibility of his situation, that his temper was ruffled, and he rose up in haste to depart, bitterly lamenting that he had ever laid his hands upon George Whitefield.' 'My Lord', said the Countess, who was an imperious dame and never happier than when bullying a Bishop, 'mark my words, when you are on your dying bed, that will be one of the few ordinations you will reflect upon with pleasure.' The Biographer of Lady Huntingdon does not fail to record what I hope was the fact, that when Bishop Benson found himself nearing his end he sent ten guineas to Whitefield and begged his prayers.

Whitefield's first London sermon was preached in St. Botolph's, Bishopsgate, on August 8, 1739.

GEORGE WHITEFIELD

At that time he was of a fair complexion, slender in figure, with blue eyes, one of which (and in this respect he resembled another famous preacher nearer our time, the late Edward Irving), was disfigured by a decided squint.

As a preacher he at once became popular and even famous, despite his youthfulness, and he soon recognized that his sphere of action was to preach the Gospel in which he believed to all he could induce to come and hear him.

He became 'a wandering voice', a missionary to a heathen England. He was to be heard almost everywhere—in churches and in the open air. He did not escape criticism—what great preachers have? They are sometimes too stiff and formal, sometimes 'cheap and vulgar'—sometimes intolerably dull, at other times far too lively. Whitefield seems never to have been dull and was occasionally very lively. His notion was that people did not require repose but stood in great need of repentance. His voice, like Mr. Spurgeon's, was exquisitely melodious.

All sorts of stories were soon afloat about his methods and the effects they produced. One very plain man, who was immensely affected by Whitefield's pulpit oratory said 'he preached like a lion'. How a lion preaches I do not know, but I imagine if a lion ever did mount a pulpit he would keep the congregation awake.

GEORGE WHITEFIELD

Lord Chesterfield was once brought by Lady Huntingdon to hear Whitefield preach and heard him describe a blind man slowly, and unwittingly, approaching a precipice—step by step, the blind man grew nearer to it—nearer and nearer, until at last Chesterfield leapt to his feet, exclaiming 'Great Heavens, he is over!' And yet Chesterfield was the politest man in London! and like all polite men hated calling attention to himself in public.

Whitefield's mission to the rich was interesting and remarkable, but his great work lay more directly amongst the poor, whom he sought out in Newgate and elsewhere, wherever he could find them. He preached a sermon to the prisoners of Newgate, taking as his text the penitent thief. It produced so great an effect upon the inmates of that great prison, that you will not be surprised to hear that the mayor and sheriffs forbade him from preaching there again. In the same way the Authorities of Bethlehem Hospital forbade Wesley to preach there again, for, said they: 'You make the inmates mad'.

One fashionable lady, the Duchess of Buckingham, who was taken by Lady Huntingdon to hear Whitefield preach, candidly avows in one of her letters her unfavourable opinion. 'Their doctrines are most repulsive, and strongly tinctured with impertinence and disrespect towards their superiors in perpetually endeavouring to level all ranks, and to do away with all distinctions. It is monstrous to be told that you have a heart as sinful as the common wretches that crawl on the earth. This is highly offensive and insulting, and I cannot but wonder your ladyship should entertain any sentiment so much at variance with high rank and good breeding.'

I think we may fairly congratulate ourselves upon having travelled far since the days of that Duchess of Buckingham; and if we have done so, it is at least as much due to Wesley and Whitefield as to Rousseau and the French Revolution.

Another thing to remember about this great preacher is that he was also a great traveller. He had crossed the Atlantic going and coming twelve times, and to cross the Atlantic in the Eighteenth Century, before the advent of Steam, was no joke and often, as Trinculo said of the accident that befell his bottle, 'an infinite loss'. Whitefield took an enormous interest in our American colonies, then a dependency of the British Crown, and in the spiritual welfare of their inhabitants. He founded an orphanage, and established friendly relations with the colonists, as they were then content to be called, though they objected to be taxed.

GEORGE WHITEFIELD

One thing here is worthy of notice. Whitefield never was an opponent of negro slavery. It did not strike him, in the circumstances, as an outrageous or ungodly institution.

Humanitariness is a plant of slow growth, and it is amazing how long a time it takes to open our long accustomed eyes to what is actually going on around us.

It must also be remembered that Whitefield's passion was for men's souls rather than for their bodies, and it is quite possible that he was taken in by the common talk amongst the pious American folk with whom he was brought in contact that it was a kindly act to remove the Children of Ham from the contamination of their heathen homes, and to introduce them, even in a state of slavery, to a Christian Land!

Something I suppose ought to be said about Whitefield's Theology, which was of the brand of John Calvin.

That Whitefield's Calvinism lent fire to his preaching and brought down many penitents to their knees can well be believed. Calvin's system was an instrument admirably adapted to work on the emotions. 'Original Sin' and 'the Corruption of Man's heart' are, as Robert Browning will tell you if you read over again his 'Gold Hair or a Legend of Pornic', still in the minds of many powerful arguments for Christianity:—

GEORGE WHITEFIELD

'I still, to suppose it true, for my part,
  See reasons and reasons; this, to begin:
'Tis the faith that launched point-blank her dart
  At the head of a lie—taught Original Sin.
The Corruption of Man's Heart.'

Nothing is immutable in this world.

'Creeds change, rites pass, no altar standeth whole.'

There are not many who may to-day have joined in singing 'Rock of Ages', know, or would perhaps care to know, that its Author, the Rev. Augustus Toplady, was one of the blackest of black Calvinists that ever drew breath in the West of England. The six volumes of his Theology are stone dead; his hymn (though his theology is not absent from it) alone survives.

Whitefield's Calvinism may have terrified many of his hearers, but it was not his particular doctrines that changed their hearts—it was the 'Rock of Ages' and the 'Cross of Christ' that impelled their conversion.

It is not to be supposed that Whitefield's sermons to-day melt the ice that binds men's hearts until they grow like steel. In this neglect he only shares the fate of those orators who were most successful in moving their audiences.

Whitefield had not Wesley's toughness of constitution and he died an old, old man at fifty-six.

There is one bit of Whitefield's writings that has always moved me. In 1767, some two years before his death, he was asked by the publishers of an Edition of all Bunyan's works to write a few words by way of preface; a practice now grown a little stale. He consented to do so, and these are his concluding words, and they will also be mine:—

'But this, I must own, more particularly endears Mr. Bunyan to my heart: he was of a catholic spirit. The want of water adult baptism with this man of God was no bar to outward Christian communion. And I am persuaded if, like him, we were more deeply and experimentally baptized into the benign and gracious influences of the blessed Spirit, we should be less baptized into the waters of strife about circumstantials and non-essentials. For being thereby rooted and grounded in the love of God we should be necessarily constrained to think and let think, bear with and forbear one another in love, and without saying, "I am of Paul, Apollos or Cephas", have but one grand, laudable, disinterested strife, namely, who should live, preach and exalt the ever-loving, altogether-lovely Jesus most! That these volumes may be blessed to beget, promote and increase such divine fruits of real and undefiled religion in the hearts, lips and lives of readers of all ranks and denominations is the earnest prayer of, Christian Reader, thy soul's well-wisher in our common Lord, George Whitefield.

'LONDON, *Jan.* 3, 1767.'

VIII

DR. CODEX

VIII

DR. CODEX

(Edmund Gibson, Bishop of London, 1723–1748.)

IN a dark corner in all well-equipped theological libraries in England there repose two folio volumes (often, *horresco referens!* bound in one), 1st edition, 1713, 2nd, much enlarged, 1761, entitled *Codex Juris Ecclesiastici Anglicani, or the Statutes, Constitutions, Canons, Rubricks, and Articles of the Church of England, methodically digested under proper heads, with a Commentary historical and juridical.*

This work, though one which no student over seventy, already turned pale by his never-resting pursuit of the question, 'What became of the Church of England after her Reformation?' can be advised to take up or down from the shelf without invoking bodily assistance, is still a book of great authority and reputation, and one that secured for its learned and methodical digester the honourable nickname, *Dr. Codex*, by which he was known by friends and foes for more than thirty years of a strenuous and virtuous life.

In his day and generation Dr. Gibson was one of the best known and most abused, both in prose and villainous rhyme, of all our Hanoverian

DR. CODEX

Prelates, and yet until the courageous and thoroughly well-informed Dr. Sykes took up his pen no regular life of Gibson had ever appeared. We cannot profess to wonder that this should be so, for in addition to all the other difficulties that beset the man who sits down to write the life of another fellow-sinner he never even saw, and who has been in his grave not far short of two hundred years, two especial difficulties confronted Dr. Sykes. The first difficulty was the Period; and the second the Man.

Dr. Gibson's period of clerical and episcopal energy was when the first two Georges and their ugly German harlots reigned over us, and when, for a number of years, Dr. Codex was credited or discredited with being Sir Robert Walpole's 'Bishop-maker'—just as many years later in our 'island-story' Lord Shaftesbury played the same rôle to that volatile yet virile statesman, Lord Palmerston.

Now, this Georgian period is not an engaging one for a clerical biography; and what makes Dr. Sykes's task the harder, is that any general reader, into whose hands this admirable book may fall, will probably have already derived a prejudice almost amounting to hatred against this very period, from the famous essay of Mark Pattison's on the 'Tendencies of Religious Thought in England, 1688–1750', which, though appearing

DR. CODEX

for the first time in 1860, between the covers of a forgotten book, now shines for ever brightly in its writer's *Collected Essays*, 2 vols., Oxford, 1889.

No single essay on such a subject has made so lasting an impression upon the mind and memory of the 'general reader', to whose continued existence we cling, although every day we come across people who seem either to have read nothing or forgotten everything.

The next difficulty in Dr. Sykes's way was the man himself. Here, again, our imaginary 'general reader' rubs his eyes, and bethinks himself of Lord Hervey's *Memoirs of the Reign of George the Second*, 2 vols., 1848, and on taking them down refreshes his memory with a vivacious and spiteful account of this very Bishop of London. Lord Hervey is not to be trusted, and Dr. Sykes has small difficulty in convicting his lordship of downright falsehood and calumny—none the less, Hervey succeeds in drawing a picture of Dr. Gibson never likely to be obliterated. Neither Dr. Gibson's period nor Dr. Gibson himself is attractive. All the more credit is therefore due to Dr. Sykes for tackling and redressing Dr. Codex, and presenting him to us as he appeared in full canonicals at St. James's.

Let us now consider Edmund Gibson a little more closely. He was born in Westmorland in 1669, and died in Bath in 1748—worn out by hard work. He came of an educated stock, and had an uncle who had married a daughter of the Lord Protector Richard Cromwell. He received a magnificent education at the humble grammar school in the parish of Bampton under a famous teacher, at a time when in Westmorland there was a good grammar school, so at least Bishop Watson, who knew the county far better than he did his own diocese of Llandaff, avers, 'under every crag'; so that when, in 1686, Gibson went up to Queen's College, Oxford, he was hailed as a miracle of learning. Gibson, whose family were somewhat impoverished, was maintained at Queen's as servitor to the Provost, a humble position of small emoluments, now divided between two Bible Clerks. 1686 was a lively time to be in residence at Oxford, for the luckless James had just begun his assault upon the Church of England in her strongest camp. He had imposed a Romanist Dean upon the Canons of Christ Church, and had dispensed the Master and Fellows of University College from all obligation to attend and perform the services of the Book of Common Prayer. He then turned his attention to Magdalen College, where his arbitrary proceedings have been read by millions with tingling ears in some of Macaulay's most animated pages.

Yet it was in this same University, so wantonly and ferociously attacked, that the twin Doctrines,

DR. CODEX

once so dear to the Church of England, and so vital to the House of Stuart, of Divine Right and Passive Obedience, that 'very doctrine of the Cross' to which the pious Ken clung so tenaciously to the last, were still held with the faith and fervour that subsequently led an Archbishop and six of his brethren on the Episcopal Bench to suffer, if not actual martyrdom, yet legal eviction from house and home, and thus to give rise to the prolonged schism of the Non-Jurors.

Queen's College must in 1686-7-8 have been an even livelier place than Oriel in Newman's time. Dr. Sykes rather smugly remarks, 'for a time Edmund Gibson was in danger of being carried away by the passion of an undiscriminating legitimism', but how legitimism can be discriminating is somewhat of a puzzle. Anyhow, Gibson was so puzzled that in 1690 he was prevented from taking his degree by his scruples about taking the necessary oaths of allegiance to William and Mary; but in the following year he had got over his doubts, being saved, so his biographer assures us, from 'an unfruitful secession by his independence of spirit and sobriety of judgment'. But the Non-Jurors did not forgive him quite so easily, and old Thomas Hearne, that sturdy Jacobite, carried his contempt so far as to deny, long after 1713, that he had ever so much as seen the *Codex Juris Anglicani*.

DR. CODEX

When once Gibson had got over his early fit of High Churchism, he left no traces of it behind him, but became at once the most confirmed of Whigs, accepted *cum animo* the Protestant Succession, and professed a passion for the Establishment and a hatred of the Church of Rome that would have satisfied Parson Thwackum. As for the Dissenters, who much to his amazement so obstinately refused to come into the fold, he was prepared to give them the full benefit of the Act of Toleration of 1689. Just so far, and not an inch farther; indeed, he marvelled at their impudence in ever demanding more.

Politically considered, Gibson's position at this period was a sound one. He regarded the Revolution Settlement, and the Establishment, as the only bulwarks against another Restoration and the Church of Rome or Infidelity. As for 'intellectual freedom', he never gave it a thought—he was not a man of ideas, he had not one in his head, but he foresaw dangers with a clear vision.

A man of strict life, with a strong dash of Puritanism in his make-up, he must have hated the two Georges from the bottom of his heart, but though it was not for him to lay critical hands on the Lord's Anointed, who had appointed him a Father in God, he tried his best to put down vice and immorality among the lower orders. He founded Societies with this end in view, and deserves great respect for his labours in establishing Charity Schools; and also for his efforts in endeavouring to propagate Christian knowledge.

Although by the bent of his mind Dr. Gibson was a dry, methodical scholar, with an antiquarian turn, he was almost forced into ecclesiastical prominence by his early acceptance of the post of domestic Chaplain to Archbishop Tenison, and as both that Archbishop and his successor Wake were for different reasons inactive, and in Wake's case for long *non compos*, Gibson, as Bishop of London, and for some considerable time *persona grata* with Walpole, became the most powerful of all the prelates.

He had a hard task. The Clergy were for the most part Tories, and half-Jacobites, and though Walpole kept the House of Commons in tolerable order, the Upper House was full of Tories, and, what was worse, of lay Whigs, as irreligious a set of dogs as ever barked at a cassock, and who treated their spiritual brethren with a contempt they took no pains to conceal. This Whig mode of treating Bishops continued down to our time, and would continue now, only there are no Whig lords left.

Then at Court, Dr. Codex fared little better. From the King nothing could be expected, though there was something in the royal suggestion that George Whitefield should be made a Bishop, but there was always Queen Caroline, Lady Sundon, and Lord Hervey plotting mischief. All three were admittedly Latitudinarians, possibly Socinians, and yet there they were for ever putting spokes into the pious chariot of Dr. Gibson, and seeking to overturn him, as at last they may be said to have succeeded in doing, a sad tale too long to tell, but it can be read in Dr. Sykes's book.

In addition to looking after the diocese of London and securing the ear of Walpole, Gibson, by Royal Warrant, had the American Colonists under his charge. The Episcopalians in America had not a Bishop among them, save for the unwelcome intrusion of two Non-Jurors, and as the Nonconformists were in a great majority, it often happened that even the Clergy were forced to send their children to be educated in dissenting Academies; where, unlike our single-school areas, there was no 'conscience clause' to protect youthful innocence. How strange to think such things could ever have been! Poor dear Episcopalians!

The subject of Dr. Gibson's activities and troubles is too large for a review, so we must end by thanking Dr. Sykes for a most interesting biography, and recommending it to the 'general reader', who though we know he is not fond of reading about Bishops should overcome this prejudice as soon as possible.

IX

DR. DODDRIDGE
(1702-1751)

IX

DR. DODDRIDGE
(1702–1751)

(*The Correspondence and Diary of Philip Doddridge, D.D.*
Edited from the original MSS. by his great-grandson, John Doddridge Humphreys, Esq. Five vols. Colburn and Bentley. 1829–1831.)

'Live while you live, the Epicure would say,
And seize the pleasures of the present day.
Live while you live, the sacred preacher cries,
And give to God each moment as it flies.
Lord—in my views, let both united be,
I live in *pleasure* when I live in *Thee*.'

THE above lines, pronounced by Dr. Johnson to be the best epigram in the English language, were written in expansion of the family motto of the Doddridges, '*Dum vivimus, vivamus*', by the celebrated Nonconformist divine whose name adorns the top of this page. And admirably well do they illustrate his literary style, talent and character.

The Doctor's (he owed his degree in Divinity to the University of Aberdeen) great-grandfather was a brother of a seventeenth-century Judge of

DR. DODDRIDGE

the King's Bench, Sir John Doddridge. The Judge was a Barnstaple man, a well-bred Devonian, educated at Exeter College, Oxford, and honoured (with his third wife) with so stately a marble tomb in the Lady Chapel of Exeter Cathedral that he can hardly fail to attract the attention of the most careless of visitors. Sir John Doddridge, living as he did under our two first Stuart Kings, was in the course of his duties, first as Law Officer and afterwards as a Judge, exposed to the charge of servility to the Crown; but as against this may be fairly set off a tribute paid to his accomplishments 'as artist, divine, civil and canon lawyer' from the glowing pen of Thomas Fuller.[1] Fuller tells us that Doddridge was called 'the *Sleeping Judge*, because he would sit on the Bench with his eyes shut, which was only a *posture of attention* to sequester his sight from distracting objects, the better to listen to what was alleged and proved'. This Judicial habit of 'sequestration' still lingers on the Bench, and is sometimes otherwise accounted for. It is a legal tradition that Sir John, who was a considerable antiquarian, and a not infrequent author, is responsible for the first edition of a legal treatise known to all lawyers, addicted to learning, as *Sheppard's Touchstone of Common Assurances*. If any of my readers are ever seized with a burning curiosity to discover 'What

[1] *Worthies of England*, 1662, p. 257.

DR. DODDRIDGE

is an Escrow', I can confidently refer him or her to *Sheppard's Touchstone*.

Philip's grandfather was one of the 'Confessors' of Nonconformity, the Rev. John Doddridge, who was ejected from his living of Shepperton in 1662, and who, as his grandson tells us, 'though he had a family of ten children unprovided for, left his living worth £200 a year rather than violate his conscience'. Dr. Calamy, in his *Nonconformist Memorial*, assures us that John Doddridge 'was of Oxford University, an ingenious man, and a scholar, an acceptable preacher and a very peaceable divine'.

I have felt it my duty to hunt through Walker's *Sufferings of the Clergy* . . . '*in the late Time of the Grand Rebellion*' to find out, if I could, how John Doddridge obtained the living of Shepperton, and who was his immediate predecessor; for quite possibly the 'peaceable' Doddridge may in Cromwellian and Presbyterian times have ejected an equally 'ingenious' member of his own University for refusing to read the then 'established Form of Public Worship'. But Walker has very little to say about the sufferings of the Clergy in Middlesex, and so my search, undertaken solely in the interests of historical truth, was in vain.

Philip Doddridge's father was a well-to-do oil merchant, who married a daughter of a Lutheran minister in Prague, who in 1626 (for the seventeenth century was everywhere a troublesome one for the proprietors of delicate consciences) had to fly his country, and pick up a living (and a very precarious one) by keeping a school at Kingston-on-Thames.

Of this marriage there was issue (*horribile dictu!*) twenty children, eighteen of whom perished in infancy, leaving the last of the brood, and one most affectionate sister, the sole survivors. When we remember that the mother of the Wesleys had nineteen children, of whom thirteen early succumbed, many thoughts, both for and against large families, crowd upon the mind.

Doddridge's biographer, the Rev. Job Orton, tells us that Philip's education was begun by his mother teaching him the Bible history from the pictures on the Dutch tiles in the chimney-corner.

The once popular *Family Expositor*, in six volumes, bears the traces, in the vivacity of its style, of this fireside origin of its author's studies.

Coming now to the subject of this paper, I must ask permission to deal with a difficult task (for the doctor was both a diffuse writer and the most volatile of divines) after the same fashion as the one he was wont to employ, in his own sermonizings, viz. by chopping my text up into four parts, or heads; and inviting you to 'lend me your ears' for a short space as I handle

DR. DODDRIDGE

Doddridge: *First*, as an Eminent Nonconformist; *Second*, as the Principal of a famous Dissenting Academy at Hinckley and Northampton; *Third*, as a Preacher, Hymn-writer, Author and Letter-writer; and *Lastly*, as a Human Being who, after an active life spent in overtaxing his strength, died in the forty-ninth year of his age at Lisbon, on the 26th of October, 1752, O.S.

Two months later, the body of another 'spent' Englishman, Henry Fielding, was laid in the same burying-ground.

And now, first, as a Nonconformist in the days of our early Hanoverian Kings.

English Nonconformity, in its modern sense, may be taken as beginning on the 24th of August, 1662. Black Bartholomew's Day. If by that date the incumbents of Church livings had not declared in writing their unfeigned assent and consent to all and everything contained and prescribed in the Book of Common Prayer, a compilation which, with the alterations made by Convocation, only made its appearance three or four days before the 24th, out they had to go. Of thirteen thousand incumbents, two thousand made this sacrifice.

This holocaust of parsons caused the very name of Subscription to be a word of horrible significance in Dissenting ears, and from that day of doom it is not too much to say that the main and most enduring difference between a Nonconformist and a Conformist was that the former regarded Subscription, whether to books, articles, canons, or formal creeds, as tyranny and bondage; whilst the latter was one who, given a pen and access to an inkpot, was ready to sign anything warranted by Convocation and enforced by Statute, without even taking the trouble of reading it. Of the countless thousands, clerics and laymen, who have since 1662 signed the Thirty-Nine Articles, how many ever first read them? and of those who did read them, how many were qualified by previous study to understand how they came to be written in the language they were.

But it would be unfair to say that of the eleven thousand of incumbents who expressed in writing their assent and consent in 1662 to a book, which in its new form hardly one hundred of them could have seen, did so because they were wholly indifferent to truth or from love of lucre or dread of losing their social position. Not at all—the great majority signed from an intense, inbred dislike of sectaries; of 'small church' groups, each stamped with the personality of its founder; of 'fancy' religions and 'fancy' prayers. And, indeed, if by a scratch of his pen a man could be sure of getting rid once for all of Ludovic Muggletons and Joanna Southcotts, and possibly of some others, 'subscription' could hardly be reckoned an unpardonable sin against Christian liberty.

DR. DODDRIDGE

But no such easy way of getting rid of what we do not like is open to us. In this matter, oaths, subscriptions, public confessions of Faith, compulsory church attendances, legal disqualifications, have been proved to be quite futile to put down religious differences. The 'pen' is here not mightier than the sword, for as a persecutor the Duke of Alva, failure as he was, was not so complete a failure as were Lord Clarendon and his restored master, in their attempts to secure uniformity of public worship and control over education.

By the time Philip Doddridge had appeared on the scene many of the old Puritanical objections to the Liturgy of the Reformed Church of England, such as the use of the surplice, the ring in matrimony, etc., had lost their force. The pious, learned and dignified leaders of Nonconformity, bewigged, begowned, and banded, of Doddridge's day, were far better representatives of the piety, sobriety and reverence for divine things within the Church of England than were the Paleys, the Warburtons, the Hurds, and the Hoadlys of the same period.

Doddridge's Nonconformity sat lightly upon him save in this one particular of Subscription. Subscribe he would not, either to the formularies of the Church of England or to the Assembly's Catechism. Had he wavered on this point he

DR. DODDRIDGE

might, with other eminent ministers, have become a Bishop.

His theology was based upon, though not deeply rooted in, what is now commonly called Calvinism, though Augustinianism would be the more correct expression; but he had been accustomed by his revered and much more learned tutor, the Reverend John Jennings, to a latitude of expression 'which the Scriptures indulge and recommend' that made 'the trammels' of subscription ever distasteful to him.

Dr. Doddridge, like Dr. Watts, was always 'suspect', in certain rigid Nonconforming quarters, on the question of the Trinity, and that the theology of both these divines was Sabellian is plain enough.

It was customary in those days to require of a young minister that he should on ordination make a confession of his faith, but as he was allowed to make it in his own language this ceremony presented no difficulty to the fluent Doddridge.

Generally speaking, I think it may be said that, apart from this question of Subscription, Doddridge might easily have been induced to conform; but as it was, he remained to the end, not indeed a 'stern', for there was nothing stern about him, but an 'unbending' Nonconformist, greatly rejoicing in his freedom from oaths and tests and catechisms.

DR. DODDRIDGE

In asking your attention to my *second* head, Doddridge as the Principal of a Dissenting Academy, I must pray your indulgence. The subject of these Dissenting Academies during the latter part of the seventeenth century and the whole of the eighteenth is one of considerable historical importance, and has never yet been treated as its position in the history of education in England deserves.[1] But to make a history of education instructive it must be written in detail, and the details of Education are apt to be uncommonly dry to all but experts. Besides, details cover pages.

As I. must be short, I will begin by giving a useful reference to an excellent, though compressed treatise on *The Dissenting Academies in England, their Rise and Progress and their Place among the Educational Systems of the Country*.[2] If further particulars are required of Dr. Doddridge's own Academy at Northampton, they will be found scattered up and down the delightful volumes of the Doctor's own correspondence.

The ecclesiastical legislation of the restored Charles was inspired (so Nonconformists have

---

[1] Much information about these Academies is to be found scattered through the eight volumes of the *Transactions of the Congregational Historical Society*.

[2] By Miss Irene Parker, M.A. (now Mrs. Parker Crane). Cambridge University Press.

DR. DODDRIDGE

always believed) by Lord Clarendon, who was a far more formidable enemy to Dissenters than ever was a much better man, Archbishop Laud, and was not content in driving out two thousand English clergymen from their homes and incomes, but pursued them wherever they went in search of an honest livelihood with a savage relentless cruelty that was never forgotten. The Act of Uniformity required that every schoolmaster and every person teaching any youth in any house or private family should subscribe a declaration that he would conform to the liturgy as by law established, and should also obtain a licence to teach from his Archbishop, Bishop, or Ordinary of the diocese. Archbishop Sheldon took care to order his Bishops to see to it that all schoolmasters, ushers and private or public teachers of youth should themselves frequent the public prayers of the Church, and cause their pupils to do the same.

Two years after the Act of Uniformity came the *Conventicle Act*, and one year later the *Five Mile Act*, and each of these statutes contained clauses aimed directly, both at the means of livelihood of the ejected ministers, and at the last remaining remnants of religious freedom and education of Nonconformists, old and young. Was it any wonder that when Queen Anne breathed her last in 1714, and the news of her

DR. DODDRIDGE

demise reached the ears of Nonconformists, as it did to many of them one Sunday morning as they were returning from the conventicles which the Revolution of 1688 had grudgingly permitted them to erect, but which were then threatened by the revived High Church party, they so far forgot themselves as to break forth in cries of exultation. So long as there was the least bit of a Stuart on the throne it was a risky thing to be a Nonconformist. Indeed, at no time has it ever been an entirely pleasant thing.

This repressive and barbarous legislature failed of its immediate purposes, which were the physical and moral starvation of the Nonconformists; for even prior to the partial toleration granted after the Revolution, it seems actually to have helped forward the cause of liberal education. It is not too much to say that from 1670 to 1800 a far better education, even in the *Trivium and Quatrivium*, to say nothing of literature, elementary science, and the principles of the Christian religion, was to be had in the numerous Dissenting Academies, soon to be found in different parts of England, than could have been obtained at either of the Universities of Oxford or Cambridge.

Miss Parker in her first appendix supplies her readers with a list of the chief Dissenting Academies in England, Presbyterian and Independent,

DR. DODDRIDGE

and appends to each seminary the names of some of their most eminent scholars.

Thus, at Islington Academy, first established (at considerable risk) in 1672, I notice the names of Calamy and Matthew Henry; whilst at Newington Green, under the tutorship of Theophilus Gale, an old Fellow of Magdalen College, Oxford, there were educated Dr. Isaac Watts, Dr. Evans, Daniel Neal (the historian of the Puritans), Henry Grove, and an Irish Archbishop of Tuam, Dr. Hort, who conformed, and was raised to this giddy eminence. I cannot help thinking Josiah Hort would have been happier had he remained content with the friendship of Dr. Watts, instead of incurring the enmity of Dr. Swift, who made the Archbishop the subject of a filthy lampoon, which may still be read by those who like such things in the fourteenth volume of Sir Walter Scott's edition of Swift.

Another student of Newington Green was Daniel de Foe, who more than once in his numerous miscellaneous writings may be found boasting of the amount of solid erudition he had acquired at Newington Green, under one of the most inspiring teachers who has ever lived in England, Charles Morton of Wadham. Whether the author of *Robinson Crusoe* and *Moll Flanders* actually knew five languages, as he asserts, need not worry us, for he certainly was the master of one, and that

DR. DODDRIDGE

one he was taught by Morton, who was the first of his conservative clan to lecture in English instead of Latin.

Morton's success as a teacher naturally called down upon him the odious attentions of the Law Officers of the Crown, and he had to desert Newington Green, and carry his great gifts to New England, where he speedily became Vice-President of Harvard.

The Academy at Tewkesbury, established in 1680, must be mentioned, not so much on account of Archbishop Secker, who probably obtained there the most valuable part of his education, but because of another Tewkesbury man, Joseph Butler, the great Bishop of Durham. Butler on conforming left Tewkesbury for Oxford, but in his letters to the famous Dr. Clarke, with whom he had begun to correspond before leaving Tewkesbury, he says that he found the Oxford studies 'dull and useless', even as did Gibbon some years later.

Some idea may be gained of the actual course of study pursued at these Dissenting Academies from reading the second appendix in Miss Parker's book, where she prints from one of Doddridge's letters [1] the course at Kibworth, where, under the tutorship of Mr. Jennings,

[1] To be found in the second volume of his *Correspondence*, p. 462.

Doddridge himself studied. The course occupied four years, and needless to say, when the pupil became the Principal, and the Academy was removed to Northampton, Doddridge, who venerated the name of Jennings, did his best to pursue the same methods.

Those Dissenting Academies were by no means confined to candidates for the ministry of any particular denomination, but were open to all who could pay the very moderate fees, and were in search of a general education, of the kind now called Secondary. Many scholars proceeding from these Academies lived to become eminent doctors and lawyers and successful and cultivated merchants, as well as archbishops, bishops, and Dissenting ministers. Nor was the theology taught in any sense sectarian, though avowedly Christian and devout. Later on, when these Academies became more and more training colleges for ministers connected with different bodies of Dissent, their distinctive glory departed.

I am now left with only two 'heads' on my hands, first the Preacher, Hymn-writer and Author; and then and lastly, the Human Being as he is revealed to us by his letters.

As a preacher Doddridge must have been both pleasant and profitable to listen to, but the easy diffuseness of his style makes quotation, at this time of day, flatly impossible. Is not fluency, as

DR. DODDRIDGE

distinguished from real eloquence, a bar to quotations? If you once begin quoting Hazlitt, you know not where to stop; but if you wish to quote from ·Doddridge, you know not, good as it all is, where to begin.

His *Family Expositor* once stood in the bookrooms of thousands of homes, when books did not abound, and was for a long period of time in daily use. Bishop Warburton, with whom Doddridge was on far too easy terms, praised the *Expositor* with apparent *gusto*, but had he ever read it? His wife, who was a pious woman, may have done so.

One of Doddridge's most popular books, *The Rise and Progress of Religion in the Soul*, is traditionally credited with the conversion of the 'celebrated' William Wilberforce, who in a note to one of the manliest and outspoken of religious treatises, the once famous *Practical View of the Prevailing Religious System of Professed Christians, contrasted with Real Christianity* (1797), mentions this work of Doddridge's, and other similar productions, in terms of warm approval and gratitude. This *Practical View* earned for Wilberforce in the House of Commons and the country the nickname of the 'Saint'.

Dr. Doddridge's *Rise and Progress* made an immediate appeal to many people, and we find the Duchess of Somerset in 1750 writing to its author as follows: "I had not the pleasure of being acquainted with any of your writings till I was at Bath three years ago, with my poor Lord, when an old acquaintance of mine, the Dowager Lady Hyndford, recommended me to read *The Rise and Progress of Religion in the Soul*; and I may with great truth assure you that I never was so deeply affected with anything I ever met with as with that book, and I could not be easy till I had given one to every servant in my house who appeared to be of a serious turn of mind." (*Correspondence*, vol. v, p. 185.)

It has always been obvious enough that the early 'Evangelicals' derived the greater part of their pious fervour from the writings of Nonconformists—Baxter, Howe, Owen, Doddridge, and others of the same school. The hungry sheep within the fold of the Establishment looked up and were fed and Christianized by 'sectarian' authors. It could hardly be otherwise, for of 'Church Principles', in the Gladstonian sense, the poor things seem never even to have heard.

As a hymn-writer Doddridge was only permitted to attain to real eminence with one or two examples. Here again his fatal gift of fluency and ease of composition played him false. A fluent hymn, like an eloquent prayer, must always be an abomination in the hearing of the Lord. Doddridge composed hundreds of hymns, of

DR. DODDRIDGE

which only two or three survive; but these are enough to keep his name alive, wherever piety meets to praise God.

> 'O God of Bethel! by whose hand
>   Thy people still are fed;
> Who through this earthly pilgrimage
>   Hast all our fathers led;

> 'Our vows, our prayers, we now present
>   Before Thy throne of grace:
> God of our Fathers, be the God
>   Of their succeeding race.'

And again:—

> 'Hark! the glad sound—the Saviour comes,
>   The Saviour promised long—
> Let every heart prepare a throne
>   And every voice a song.'

Dr. Watts, save when paraphrasing a Psalm of David, never comes up to Doddridge at his best.

I cannot pass away from Doddridge's books without saying something about the one of them that attained a greater popularity in the outside world, and has been more frequently reprinted than any of his other publications. I refer to the book called *Some Remarkable Passages in the Life of Colonel James Gardiner*, published in 1747, which has often been reprinted by the Religious Tract Society.

DR. DODDRIDGE

Colonel Gardiner (1688–1745) was as gallant a soldier as ever fought and swore in Flanders. He was desperately wounded at Ramillies (1706), and some ten years afterwards entered Paris, in great state, as Master of the Horse to our Ambassador, Lord Stair. It was his fate to die a hero's death at Prestonpans in the unhappy affair of the Forty-Five.

In his early days in Paris the Colonel led a loose life, and it was whilst waiting to keep an unlawful assignation with the wife of a surgeon that, in order to while away the time, he took up a pious book, once given him by his mother or his aunt, either Gurnall's *Christian Armour* or Watson's *Christian Soldier*, and whilst thus occupied he underwent the experience which Doddridge, who had it from the Colonel's own lips, for they had become friends and correspondents, describes as follows:—

'He thought he saw an unusual blaze of light fall on the book while he was reading, which he at first imagined might happen by some accident in the candle. But lifting up his eyes, he apprehended to his extreme amazement that there was before him, as it were suspended in the air, a visible representation of the Lord Jesus Christ upon the Cross, and was impressed as if a voice had come to him, to this effect, though he was not confident as to the very words, "Oh, sinner, did I suffer this for thee, and are these the returns?" But whether this was an audible

DR. DODDRIDGE

voice, or only a strong impression on his mind, he did not seem very confident—though to the best of my remembrance he rather judged it to be the former. Struck with so amazing a phenomenon as this, there remained hardly any life in him, so that he sank down in his chair and continued, he knew not how long, insensible.'

From that time forward the Colonel led a godly, sober and pure life.

There are usually two versions of out-of-the-way occurrences. Colonel Gardiner, though the last man in the world to boast of his prowess on the field of battle, was not equally reticent on the subject of his remarkable conversion, and was in the habit of recounting it to different companies, composed of very different auditors. Dr. Doddridge, who—though a credulous person in such matters—was a man whose verbal veracity cannot be questioned, assures us that he tells the Colonel's story as it was told to him by the Colonel himself. But in the interesting autobiography of Dr. Alexander Carlyle (Blackwood, 1860), an equally veracious, though most secular-minded Presbyterian divine, who lived so far down as 1805, tells us that though Colonel Gardiner told him the story of his conversion on three or four distinct occasions, and dwelt on the assignation and the pious book, he never so much as mentioned either the vision or the voice.

DR. DODDRIDGE

As Dr. Carlyle, though a minister of the Kirk of Scotland, was a sceptic of the school of David Hume, and would not have believed a word about either the vision or the voice, the Colonel may have concluded that it would be useless to mention them. On the other hand, without the vision and the voice the story is one hardly worth the trouble of such frequent repetitions.

However, from the Colonel's point of view, his conversion was the most important matter, and on that Dr. Carlyle throws no manner of doubt.

Sixty years ago this story, as narrated by Doddridge, was still frequently discussed in pious circles.

The careful reader of *Waverley* will not need to be reminded that Colonel Gardiner appears as Waverley's commanding officer. "In person he was tall and handsome and active, though somewhat advanced in life. In early years he had been what is called, by way of palliative, a very gay young man, and strange stories were circulated about his sudden conversion from doubt, if not infidelity, to a serious, if not enthusiastic, turn of mind. It was whispered that a supernatural communication, of a nature obvious even to the exterior senses, had produced this wonderful change, and though some mentioned the proselyte as an enthusiast, none hinted at his

DR. DODDRIDGE

being a hypocrite. This singular and mystical circumstance gave Colonel Gardiner a peculiar and solemn interest in the eyes of the young soldier.' (*Waverley*, chap. vii.) See also *Varieties of Religious Experience*, by William James, p. 369.

I have now come to the end, for I find it impossible in the space at my disposal to deal with Doddridge as a Human Being. He is too *diffuse* to be distilled into an epigram or dismissed in a paragraph. You must read his letters as he wrote them—at length. As a letter-writer he has great merits. His merriment is not parsonic, though always pious.

That Doddridge was a 'great lover' is soon made manifest to any reader of his correspondence. Fortunately for him, he lived in days when a large amount of kissing pretty women was allowed to pass unrebuked. Erasmus tells us in his letters how he appreciated this English custom of frequent salutation. He could not have appreciated it more than Dr. Doddridge. This agreeable habit or custom may have lingered longer among the Scotch than it has with us, for certainly, if Mrs. Thomas Carlyle is to be credited, Lord Jeffery was accustomed to embrace her with an animated vivacity that even Doddridge could not have surpassed.

Doddridge's love affairs are narrated by him at Richardsonian length, though in a vein of

DR. DODDRIDGE

high spirits and genuine humour. His courtships, though sometimes prolonged, were not (with one exception) successful, but he bore his disappointments with Christian resignation; and when he did marry he made the best of husbands, and to the end of his life, whenever he was away from home, as he frequently was on his preachings, he bombarded his wife with letters in which the ardour of the lover was never lost in the dull composure of the husband. But he continued a flirt to the end.

The pair had nine children, but when the Doctor died he left behind him only his widow, one son and three daughters. The son, though he began well, was not a success, though he lived to be forty-seven. One of the three daughters married and had children; the other two remained unmarried, and died far advanced in years. The widow survived her volatile husband thirty-nine years, and died in 1790.

No 'eminent Christian', and such Doddridge most emphatically was, better exemplified in his life the truth and beauty of his own lines:—

'Lord, in my views let both united be,
I live in *pleasure* when I live in *Thee*.'

X

CLERGYMEN AND CHURCHWARDENS IN THE EIGHTEENTH CENTURY

X

CLERGYMEN AND CHURCHWARDENS IN THE EIGHTEENTH CENTURY

(1) The Diary of Thomas Turner of East Hoathley, 1754–1765.

(2) The Diary of the Rev. James Woodforde, 1758 onwards.

(3) The Diary of the Rev. William Jones of Broxbourne, 1777–1821.

THE great Mr. Congreve begins his single contribution to Mr. Steele's *Tatler* (No. 42, 1709) after the following engaging fashion:—

'The Discourse happen'd this evening to fall upon the characters drawn in Plays, and a Gentleman remark'd that there was no method in the World of shewing the Taste of an Age, or Period of Time so good as by the Observations of the persons represented in Comedies.'

A very sensible remark to be made by a stray gentleman in a London coffee-house in 1709, and the good sense of it applies with equal force to the Diaries of past days when honestly kept by honest men.

CLERGYMEN AND CHURCHWARDENS

Damns, it was said long ago, have had their day, though since the appearance of the Labour Party in the House of Commons, they have shown a tendency to reappear in Parliament; but whatever may be the truth about damns, there is no doubt of the exceeding popularity of Diaries at the present time.

It does not seem to matter very much how dull the Diary may prove to be, nor in the least by whom it was kept; popular it is sure to be if a work of good faith, and an honest record of a daily life led almost anywhere.

Publishers, though sniffing at sermons, and surfeited with Novels, snatch greedily at Diaries, and may be found with their usual effrontery asserting on the dust-covers that these publications of theirs cannot fail to remind the reader of either Pepys or Evelyn, two very different men who have become as much the sponsors of English Diaries as erst were Herodotus and Thucydides the Fathers of History.

It is perhaps possible that the popularity of Diaries is to be accounted for by the growing distaste for 'standard' histories. Had Smollett and Hume (yoked together by the 'Trade'), Macaulay and Froude been included in the Canon of Holy Scripture, their authority could hardly be more harshly scrutinized than they are to-day by the younger race of Students.

IN THE EIGHTEENTH CENTURY

Diaries, unless faked, make none of the pretensions of the standard historian. They do not profess to be History, not even of their own times, but let you into the secret of the daily lives of your predecessors, how they ate and drank and swore, and were either the pride of their parents or broke their hearts (perhaps really they did neither but only thought they did), and this in a familiar style that convinces the reader that behind the stage-arras of history there throbbed such a thing as human life.

It is hard to fathom the depths of the scepticisms that lurk in the recesses of our breasts. We require the Sphinx to convince us of Antiquity, and we are grateful to the Arch of Titus for giving us such positive assurance that the Siege of Jerusalem actually 'went through the formality of taking place'. Old-fashioned folk who cling to the verbal inspiration of the Bible clutch greedily at any fresh evidence indicating that once upon a time there was a great Flood. It is sometimes hard to believe in the reality of History so bedevilled has the Muse been by the picturesque and the partisan historian.

We can assure the suspicious reader that in no one of the three Diaries named above will he be able to discover any traces of the picturesque or the partisan historian.

The earliest of these Diarists, Mr. Thomas

CLERGYMEN AND CHURCHWARDENS

Turner, was first a village schoolmaster (hence his taste for reading), then a village shopkeeper, a parish overseer, and a Churchwarden in a Sussex parish, where he lived on terms of friendly joviality with the Vicar, one Mr. Porter. Mr. Turner's Diary makes a slender volume of a hundred pages. His dates are 1754 to 1765, and the Diary ends abruptly on his second marriage.

The second Diary is presented to us in three nobly printed volumes (and a fourth is promised), proceeding from the Press of the University to which the Diarist belonged.

The Rev. James Woodforde, whose Diary begins in 1758, was in every sense an Oxford man, having been, though by no means a learned man, both a scholar and a Fellow of New College, and the occupant of a College Living in Norfolk for thirty years.

All three Diaries are truthful as to facts, and make no effort to conceal or minimize the frailties of their writers. As we read we see before us the lives of a Churchwarden and of two Vicars as led during a remarkable period of English history.

Mr. Woodforde's Diary has been hailed with something not unlike enthusiasm, if a word he would have disliked may be here employed, by genuine book-readers—I mean by those who read books for enjoyment and not for pay.

IN THE EIGHTEENTH CENTURY

Against the verdict of such men it would be absurd to appeal. We confess to having felt surprise when told that good Churchmen, the inheritors of the Tractarian Movement, have been so moved by this *Diary of a Country Parson* as to have been seen carrying it away under their arms to add to their libraries; though probably not to put it on the same shelf with George Herbert or John Keble.

The Third Diary, that of the Rev. William Jones (1777–1821), reveals a character of quite another type from either the Village Schoolmaster and Churchwarden or the Fellow of New College. Mr. Jones's Diary illustrates with vividness and extreme vivacity what may be called the Methodistical strain in the Church of England during the eighteenth century.

We never should have heard anything of these three Diarists, but for their Diaries. All of them may be called good men, and no one (considering how it is only by their confessions or admissions we have got to know anything about them at all) has the right, even were he churl enough to wish to do so, to throw a stone at any one of the three. As, however, Diaries when published are meant to be read, and when these Diaries do come to be read, it cannot be denied that the layman's Diary is the Diary of a Drunkard, the Vicar of Weston's Diary is the Diary of a Glutton, and the

CLERGYMEN AND CHURCHWARDENS

Vicar of Broxbourne's Diary is the Diary of a hen-pecked Husband.

To prove these allegations as they could be proved up to the hilt would be to infringe the law of copyright, and require a quotation from almost every page, and in Mr. Woodforde's case, an accumulation of stomachic details which however curious when found in their contexts, must when torn from them excite disgust, and even demand some of those remedies for nausea which the reverend Diarist was always careful to keep by his bedside.

In the same way the drunkenness of the Churchwarden, and the relations of Mr. Jones with his wife, are not things to be insisted upon apart from the lives of excellent men who, despite their failings and misfortunes, were quite as lovable creatures as are any of the characters in Fielding or Smollett.

The Churchwarden, though he had enjoyed none of the advantages of a College life, had a far more decided tincture of letters than the Vicar of Weston, whose favourite tincture was of quite another character. Mr. Turner was a great reader and had a sensible taste. A few extracts from the beginnings of his Diary ought to be given:—

'*Sunday, Feb.* 8 (1754).—As I by experience find how much more conducive it is to my health, as well as pleasantness and serenity to my mind, to live in a low, moderate rate of diet, and as I know I shall never be able to comply therewith in so strickt a manner as I should chuse, by the unstable and over-easyness of my temper, I think it therefore fit to draw up Rules of proper Regimen, which I do in the manner and form following, which I hope I shall always have the strictest regard to follow, as I think they are not inconsistent with either religion or morality.

'If I am at home, or in company abroad, I will never drink more than four glasses of strong beer: one to toast the King's health, the second to the Royal Family, the third to all friends, and the fourth to the pleasure of the company. If there is either wine or punch, never upon any terms or perswasion to drink more than eight glasses, each glass to hold no more than half a quarter of a pint.

' "Clarissa Harlow" I look upon as a very well-wrote thing, tho' it must be allowed it is too prolix. The author keeps up the character of every person in all places; and as to the manner of its ending, I like it better than if it had terminated in more happy consequences.

'My wife read to me that moving scene of the funeral of Miss Clarissa Harlow. Oh, may the Supreme Being give me grace to lead my life in such a manner as my exit may in some measure be like that divine creature's.

'*Wednesday*, *Feb*. 22.—About four o'clock p.m. I walked down to Whyly. We played at bragg the first part of the even. After ten we went to supper on four boiled chicken, four boiled ducks, minced veal, sausages, cold roast goose, chicken pasty, and ham. Our company, Mr. and Mrs. Porter, Mr. and Mrs. Coates, Mrs. Atkins, Mrs. Hicks, Mr. Piper and wife, Joseph Fuller and wife, tho. Fuller and wife, Dame Durrant, myself and wife, and Mr. French's family. After supper our behaviour was far from that of serious, harmless mirth; it was down-right obstreperous, mixed with a great deal of folly and stupidity. Our diversion was dancing or jumping about, without a violin or any musick, singing of foolish healths, and drinking all the time as fast as it could be well poured down; and the parson of the parish was one among the mixed multitude. . . . About three o'clock, finding myself to have as much liquor as would do me good, I slipt away unobserved, leaving my wife to make my excuse. Though I was very far from sober, I came home, thank God, very safe and well, without even tumbling; and Mr. French's servant brought my wife home, at ten minutes past five.

'*Sunday, Aug.* 5.—I spent most part of to-day in going to and from Halland, there being a public day, where there was to dine with his Grace the Duke of Newcastle, the Earls of Ashburnham and Northampton, Lord Viscount Gage, the Lord Abergavenny, and the two judges of assize, and a great number of gentlemen, there being, I think, upwards of forty coaches, chariots, etc. . . . I came home about seven, not thoroughly sober.'

It would be unkind to give further extracts

IN THE EIGHTEENTH CENTURY

narrating, with touching sincerity, his quarrels with his first wife, who shared his convivial, if not his literary, tastes. Her faults, like Falstaff's lies, were gross and palpable, but, when she comes to die, her husband mourns over her with sincerity, recognizing, as indeed well he might, that there were shortcomings on both sides.

Mr. Porter, parson of the parish who buried Mr. Turner's first wife and married him to his second, was a scandalous ill-liver, and yet had the effrontery, the Sunday after a drunken orgy, to preach one of the best sermons Turner (who was an excellent judge of a sermon, and records the fact that he once read five of Tillotson's on one day) had ever heard, on the sin of swearing!

Turner's Diary ends abruptly after his second marriage (in 1765) to a lady he thus describes:—

'As to her person, I know it's plain (so is my own) but she is cleanly. She is, I think, a well-made woman, though not a learned lady nor a gay one, but, I trust, she is good-natured. As to her fortune, I shall one day have something considerable.'

Breaking the Diary habit did not hasten Mr. Turner's end, for he lived on for more than twenty-four years, and had seven children by the lady so well described. We part from the good fellow without emotion. His great failing robbed his life of dignity and self-respect, but he had within him the makings of a pious Churchwarden.

Having passed over the one infirmity of the Churchwarden of Hoathley as lightly as possible, it would be an offence against the cloth to dwell at greater length than I have already done upon the besetting sin of the Vicar of Weston.

However it came about that James Woodforde was able to write himself down a Scholar and Fellow of New College we are not told, yet that he could, when put to it, stand some sort of an examination the following extract proves:—

'*May* 23 (1763).—I went this afternoon at five o'clock to L. L. L. to Mr. Hewish the Bishop of Oxford's Chaplain, before whom I was examined for deacon's orders, and I came off very well. I was set over in the middle of the fifth chapter of St. Paul to the Romans, and construed the chapter quite to the end. I was quite half-an-hour examining. He asked a good many hard and deep questions. I had not one question that "Yes" or "No" would answer.'

On the 28th of May he subscribed to The Thirty-nine Articles, and in the following day was ordained deacon by the Bishop of Oxford, and partook of the Sacrament in the Cathedral. On the 1st of June he took his B.A. degree, and then, as was usual, he and four other bachelors treated, in the Bachelors' Common Room of New,

IN THE EIGHTEENTH CENTURY

twenty-seven friends to dinner with wine, and, after dinner, to supper, with wine and punch all the evening. The Diary then proceeds:—

'I sat up in the B.C.R. till after twelve o'clock and then went to bed and at three in the morning had my outward doors broken open, my glass door broke, and pulled out of bed and brought into the B.C.R. where I was obliged to drink and smoak but not without a good many words. Peckham broke my doors, being very drunk, although they were open, which I do not relish of Peckham very much.

'*June* 2.—Several of our Fellows went at four o'clock in the morning for Stors, and all drunk, some in phaeton, some in a buggy, and some on horseback. I went as far as Weston-on-the-Green with them upon my Grey, and then returned home and was home by nine o'clock in the morning and breakfasted in my room.'

I gave this extract to show, what is indeed the truth, that the Vicar, unlike the poor, struggling Churchwarden, was never tempted by strong drink, or was able to resist the temptation. The sin that most easily beset him lay in another direction.

None-the-less, it was this parson's misfortune, from the very beginning of his clerical days, to be compelled to associate with relatives of obnoxious habits, notably his brother John—

CLERGYMEN AND CHURCHWARDENS

'a madcap ruffian and a swearing Jack', who, to the sorrow of his parents, inhabited the paternal parsonage of Ansford in Somerset, where, for some years after his ordination, James Woodforde lived, whilst serving curacies in the neighbourhood.

We forbear to supply the extracts that exhibit this noisy, drunken blackguard disgracing his father's parsonage, but the fact that our quiet, dignified, well-behaved parson was pursued through life with ill-living relatives and a veritable son of Belial for a brother, with whom he put up with only too great toleration, should not be overlooked in this Diary of a quiet life.

Being sworn off the subject of Parson Woodforde's unsubdued appetite for food, there is little left to say.

Woodforde was one of the most kind-hearted, wide-minded, and generous of men. He scattered his shillings with free hands, and his compassion extended to all classes of the community. I will give but one example. Being in Bath (Bath and Yarmouth divided equally his affections), and whilst taking a walk one evening in the Fields, he met two girls, the eldest about seventeen, the youngest about fifteen,

'both common prostitutes even at that early age. I gave them some good advice to consider the End of Things. I gave them 0–1–0!'

IN THE EIGHTEENTH CENTURY

It is meat and drink to me to meet a priest like this!

Our Vicar was never married, his niece, Nancy, keeping house for him at Weston. They got on together capitally; though we do read how, on one occasion, Nancy sulked for twenty-four hours and refused to eat anything because her uncle had told her she 'eat too much'. Satan rebuking sin was evidently more than his housekeeper could stand.

The careful reader of this Diary will find more in it than gastronomy. Thomas Love Peacock, in his great "Essay on Gastronomy and Civilization" (see the 9th volume of the Holliford edition of Peacock's Works, Constable), is to be found lamenting

'that of the vast numbers of recorded and narrated festivals, it is in most instances impossible to obtain the bill of fare.'

The creator of Dr. Opimian, had he been favoured to read our parson's Diary in manuscript, would have been the first to acknowledge that the Vicar of Weston is not open to this charge of undue reticence on so important a theme.

But, quite apart from food, this Diary contains many curious facts, throwing light upon some of the habits and customs of the last century but one. For example, the Vicar of Weston lived on the same easy terms with the smuggler who supplied his cellar with brandy and gin as did the Laird of Ellangowan with Dirk Hatteraick.

As for the annual tithe feasts, which are only too faithfully described, viler orgies could hardly have occurred more frequently in the days of the worship of Odin and Thor.

Woodforde's Bishop was always bothering him to be supplied with lists of the Papist recusants in his parish, though, so far as the parson knew, there were none. An inquiry as to the number of sober Christians there were dwelling within the same boundaries would have been more to the purpose, and possibly might have elicited the same reply.

The Diary of the Rev. William Jones, as a study of a particular kind of parson at the end of the eighteenth and the beginning of the nineteenth century, is the most informing of the three.

No enemy of the Church of England can accuse this Diarist of the sin of 'gentility', or of bowing down in the House of Rimmon, or blinking his eyes to the impieties in Church or State. For a good Bishop, like Dr. Porteus, Bishop of London, who gave him, after twenty years' service as a curate on £60 a year, the living of Broxbourne, and on one occasion 'refreshed my pocket with a £10 check on his Bankers', Mr. Jones cannot

IN THE EIGHTEENTH CENTURY

speak too highly, and on the Bishop's death records in the Diary his 'translation to Heaven'; but for bad bishops, such as the infamous Dr. Crigan, Bishop of Sodor and Man, who obtained the See from the Duchess of Athol by dressing himself up as an old and broken-down divine, hardly likely to last six weeks, whereas he lasted twenty-four years; and that scandalous absentee prelate Frederick Augustus Hervey, the Bishop of Derry, afterwards Lord Bristol, our Diarist simply revels in abuse.

Nor was this anger the rage of a disappointed man, himself seeking preferment. It was the genuine indignation of a sincere Christian.

Born in 1755 at Abergavenny, of poor parents, from whom, I suppose, he inherited both his black Calvinism and his lively and over-friendly disposition, ever at war with his creed, young Jones took to his books, and after helping as an assistant teacher at the Grammar School of his native place, obtained some sort of a bursary or sizar-ship at Jesus College, Oxford, where he proceeded in 1777. His life at Oxford was not voluptuous and very unlike that of Mr. Woodforde's at New. It was in truth a miserable, half-starved existence, and he kept company more with pious old women belonging to the Town than with the 'gemmen', as he calls them, of the Gown. He says that the coffee-house an undergraduate frequented counted in his life far more than his College. Nevertheless, his wits being always on the alert, and sharpened by his poverty, he managed to pick up the crumbs of a clerical education as they fell from the sizar's table, and devoured them more greedily than ever did the future Vicar of Weston in the fashionable society of New.

To the end of his days Jones had his Latin tags on the tip of his tongue, and was able to increase his narrow stipend by taking in foreign pupils, Swiss and German, much to the satisfaction of his thrifty wife, who always kept her husband's nose to the grindstone.

His Calvinism and Methodistical turn of mind, combined with his poverty and general shabbiness, made him out of place even in Jesus, but his common sense rescued him from expulsion as 'an enthusiast', and his good steady conduct obtained for him, on the recommendation of the Principal of the College, a tutorship for the four young sons of an Attorney-General for Jamaica, whither he went, joyfully enough, for he hated Oxford, and without taking his degree, in February, 1778.

In Jamaica Jones remained for two years, and later in life he declared them to be his two happiest. You certainly would not have thought them happy years, whilst reading his account of his

IN THE EIGHTEENTH CENTURY

sojourn in that 'suburb of Hell' as he describes it in his Diary.

His account of the Island is worth reading for the information he gives. It certainly is a very beastly bit of history, even when every allowance is made, and in reading the Diary of a black Calvinist great allowance must always be made 'for the wind'.

Jones was no great Humanitarian—how can a Calvinist be a great Humanitarian?—and at times you find him declaring that the slaves were happier than the dissolute and impious whites, but at other times he records sights and sounds which are horrible enough. The vocabulary of a Calvinistic Diary is not entirely to be trusted, nor is such language as rose habitually to Mr. Jones's lips and flowed easily from his pen a truth-telling medium—but allowing for this, his Account of social life in Jamaica, 1778-1780, gives this Diary of his an historical interest, though in its humanitarian aspect it contrasts unfavourably with Monk Lewis's well-known Diary of his visit to his West Indian Estates.

On his return to England, Jones went back to Oxford to take his degree and orders. His B.A. Examination presented no difficulties. He does not appear to have been asked a single question, which was perhaps as well, for he had not read any book in Greek or Latin preparatory for it. He managed to get a few pupils at Oxford with whom he read *Locke on Education*. He then began looking about for clerical work, and a friend of his, and he had always good friends, wished to procure him a lectureship at Enfield, and also most kindly recommended him to take a wife, and introduced him for that purpose to an elderly Miss M. P. with a snug fortune of her own.

'M. P. appeared. I thought her a thousand times more beautiful and charming than ever my warmest imagination had represented.' But then— 'She seems to be an utter stranger to God, and yet I fondly think that I could be happy with her. Yet were I to marry her, what distress might it not occasion? The more I loved her, the more would it pierce my soul to think that I was embracing in my bosom one who, perhaps, must be after this life everlastingly separated from me. . . . But what am I dreaming of? Is it not time to awake?'

But again:—

'Her fortune I find amounts to what Mr. C. mentioned (£14,000). Handsome as it is her present expenses are equal to it. Her person is pleasing. All these circumstances considered I wonder no offer has been made which she has thought proper to accept. Now she has passed her prime she may be disposed to notice, or

IN THE EIGHTEENTH CENTURY

perhaps accept proposals which a few years ago she would have rejected with disdain. But she knows not God. Nay she despises religion. How then can I have a thought of her? Better perhaps for me to marry a decent woman, who fears God, with a small fortune or without any. May the Lord direct me!"

Here was a pretty quandary for a Calvinist, not to say a Christian, to find himself in.

Sunday, Feb. 4, 1781.—'Recd. this morning a letter from Mr. H. He informs me that Miss P. is just going to change her name. 'Tis now too late, and little worth my while, to be sorry for what passed about three months ago. It will however I hope' (*five lines erased*).

Having escaped Miss M. P., Jones fell to the lot of Theodosia Jessopp, a lawyer's daughter of very respectable family, who is thus described:—

'My *dear* wife is a lawyer's daughter, and possesses such a wonderful volubility of speech, such a miraculous power of twisting and twisting every argument to her own interests that I am no match for her *High Mightiness*. She right well knows how "to puzzle right and varnish wrong". No Old Bailey solicitor throughout the Kingdom better knows this sublime art.'

This pair of lovers lived together from Trinity Sunday, 1781, to October 12, 1821, when the husband died. Nine children were born of the union, and (so it would appear) loved both their parents equally well. We must not take sides with either.

Amongst his journals was one entitled *A Book of Domestic Lamentations*, which, so it appears from repeated references made to it in the printed Journal, contained a record of his matrimonial woes and grievances, but as Mrs. Jones survived her husband six years, we are not surprised to be told that it has long disappeared. There was also a *Journal of Health*, of considerable length, concerned with his own and his parishioners' ailments. This also has gone, and we miss it more than we do the *Lamentations*, for the Curate and Vicar of Broxbourne took a great interest in the corpses of the 'poor worms', as he called his parishioners; and the Faculty could not fail to have learnt something from his curious details.

We could pleasantly pursue Mr. Jones through his forty years of duty at Broxbourne and Hoddesdon, where he had good friends whom he blessed, and knavish enemies (notably one Rogers) whom he roundly curses.

He had great difficulty in collecting personally his tithes in kind, and was often treated with the utmost rudeness, for as he records, 'the very word *tithe* has ever been as unpleasing and odious to farmers especially, as the word cuckoo to the married ear'.

Occasionally his good nature led him into financial difficulties, as when, behind his wife's back, he lent £30 to a young West Indian who lived in Broxbourne Lodge, and had the impudence to stand for the County in 1806 against two such well-worn Whigs and Hertfordshire gentlemen as the Hon. Edward Spencer Cowper and Mr. Nicholas Calvert. The upstart was handsomely thrashed.

But financially, what with pupils and a thrifty wife, he managed to scrape along, and he had behind him a friendly banker who helped him with his small investments, and was plentifully rewarded with prayer and praise.

Jones was an abstemious man, forgoing, though not without suffering, both snuff and tobacco, though at times, midst 'social noise' and in worldly company, for he loved a dinner-party when he could get one, he forgot himself so far as to talk 'foolishly'—i.e. wittily, for he was a witty man full of agreeable fancies. It is easy to see that at the bottom of his heart he was a good fellow and a sincere Christian. As a type of an English clergyman he has probably for ever disappeared.

XI

THE BIRTHPLACE OF 'PAMELA' AND 'CLARISSA'

XI

THE BIRTHPLACE OF 'PAMELA' AND 'CLARISSA'[1]

IN 1741 there appeared anonymously in London an octavo volume bearing the following lengthy and (to us) forbidding title, which must, however, be given, for it is the birthplace of world-famous novels:—

>Letters
>written To and For
>Particular Friends
>on the most
>Important Occasions
>Directing not only the Requisite
>Style and Forms
>to be Observed in Writing
>Familiar Letters;
>But how to
>Think and Act, Justly and Prudently,
>in the
>Common Concerns
>of
>Human Life
>Containing
>One hundred and seventy-three Letters
>none of which were ever before Published.

[1] *Familiar Letters on Important Occasions*, by Samuel Richardson. With an Introduction by Brian W. Downs, Fellow of Christ's College, Cambridge.
Richardson, by Brian W. Downs.

THE BIRTHPLACE OF

This original volume (now reprinted for the first time since the century before last) owes its origin (as in truth do many better books) to the suggestive minds of two once well-known Printers (Mr. Charles Rivington and Mr. John Osborn), who, laudably anxious to keep their presses at work, entreated Richardson (in his own words) 'to write for them a little volume of letters in a common style, on such subjects as might be of use to those country readers who were unable to indite for themselves. "Will it be any harm", said I, "in a piece you want to be written so low, if we should instruct them how they should think and act in common cases as well as indite?" They were the more urgent with me to begin this little volume for this hint'.

It is hard to read these simple words of an honest tradesman without experiencing the same emotions that rise within us when we stand by the side of the origin of great rivers, such as the Mersey or the Clyde, which we know are destined to carry to the great ocean, and to the ports of the world, the heavily freighted ships of our Mercantile Marine. On this moving though simple text Mr. Downs has constructed a fascinating Introduction of fifteen pages, full of learning and reading, and all the more delightful because hardly to be looked for in a volume containing letters addressed to an imaginary young man 'on

'PAMELA' AND 'CLARISSA'

too soon keeping a horse', or from a young woman 'recommending a wet-nurse'! But when we remember we are visiting the birthplace of *Pamela* and *Clarissa*, nothing need surprise us. Mr. Downs traces back to Egypt and the Pharaohs the useful habit of collecting precedents to be employed on 'Important Occasions'.

Experience, both as an articled clerk to a solicitor and in later life, as a draftsman of clauses in Bills to be submitted to a partisan Parliament, has taught me that there is usually somewhere in existence a draft for almost everything. You seldom are required to start anything quite fresh. Whether there were previous drafts for the Ten Commandments we dare not say—there certainly were for the Thirty-Nine Articles. Cassiodorus (so Mr. Downs tells us), *circa* A.D. 537, collected seventy-two drafts of public documents; and in the *Bibliothèque Nationale* in Paris is deposited a long correspondence, previous to and during litigation between an Archdeacon of Chartres and his Bishop, to serve as models for future ecclesiastical strife.

When printing came along, the demand for precedents, even in familiar letters, was stimulated, and in Venice in 1487 there appeared a *Formularia de epistole vulgare*, said on the title-page to have been compiled by Bartolommea Minatore, though, says Mr. Downs, the British

Museum thinks fit to assign it to C. Landino. We may be sure good Mr. Richardson derived no assistance from these early predecessors in the same line of business.

Englishmen have ever loved precedents, even in their love-letters, and so, Mr. Downs tells us, our earliest collector of Forms for Letters appeared in 1568, in the person of William Fulwood, in his *Enemie of Idleness, teaching the manner and stile how to endite, compose, and write all sorts of Epistles and Letters*. The book was in four sections, and the last is made up of love-letters, not only in prose, but in verse. This was before the date of actions for breach of promise of marriage.

In our Editor's opinion Nicolas Breton is the first ancestor in the direct line of Richardson, for his *Post with a Packet of Mad Letters*, which appeared about 1600, had a great run that continued down to the date of Richardson's birth, and may therefore have become known to him. Breton's compilation contained 153 letters.

Mr. Downs pursues his subject through the eighteenth century, but we can follow him no farther; only remarking that he calls our attention to the fact that the habit of telling a fictitious story by means of inventing letters and attributing them to the characters was, if not actually started in France, greatly favoured there, lending itself as it did to erotic writing. 'The finest purely French

'PAMELA' AND 'CLARISSA'

token of this mintage, Marivaux's *Marianne* (1731–41), had just been completed when Richardson finished his commission for the *Familiar Letters*' (see Introduction, page xxi).

Tearing ourselves away from the Introduction, we approach the *Familiar Letters* themselves. We say at once that we cannot honestly press them upon the turned-up noses of those non-Richardsonians who are doomed to go to their graves preferring *Tom Jones* and *Amelia* to *Clarissa* and *Grandison*. Yet even these stony-hearted readers may, as lovers of literature, deign to cast a glance over the pages of a Collection of Letters, which though they will certainly provoke many smiles, have a place in the genesis of genius.

Mr. Downs singles out three of the Letters (Nos. 62, 138, 139) which relate to attempts made to destroy the virtue of servant-girls, and reveal in homely language the risks Innocence runs both in town and country, and also shows what a strong hold these dangers had got upon the mind and conscience of the author of *Pamela*. Otherwise and for the most part these Letters deal with less tragic incidents in the common concerns of human life; as, e.g., the one addressed 'To a Gentleman of Fortune who has Children, dissuading him from a Second Marriage with a Lady much older than Himself' (No. 140). An admirable letter!

This Collection does contain one Letter (No. 176) which is throughout composed in a style, coarse and strong, and abounding in vulgar expressions; a style which all Richardsonians will at once recognize with pride as being truly his, whenever he thought the occasion demanded it. This is the style that so annoyed the prim Southey, who reserved all his strong language for those who had the assurance to differ from him in the politics of his later days—and would also, we feel sure, greatly surprise a late Home Secretary, who has probably always regarded Richardson as a very ladylike author who could safely be recommended to his 'little ones'.

Even before the *Familiar Letters* was ready for the press, *Pamela* was begun, and *Pamela* begat *Clarissa*, and *Clarissa* begat *Sir Charles Grandison*, and there, to the grief of a few, and the relief of many, the propagation ceased. But now, it is made plain to us, that by devoting so much of our space to Mr. Downs's Introduction to Richardson's *Familiar Letters*, we have left ourselves no room to expatiate on the merits of his book on Richardson himself. These merits are great. If the reader begins the book at the end, and reads the Index first, he will at once perceive how well the biographer is equipped for his task. Mr. Downs's knowledge of those who are often somewhat contemptuously described as 'the old

'PAMELA' AND 'CLARISSA

Novelists of the Eighteenth Century' can only be described, in the unavoidable language of Dickens, as 'extensive and peculiar', for not only does he know the names of the novelists, men and women alike (for this mere Index knowledge 'turns no student pale'), but he knows and tells you the contents of their stories, and discriminates between them most judiciously. He thinks highly of *Betty Thoughtless*, and speaks up for Tom Brown's *Lindamara*, though this Tom Brown of 'facetious memory' must not for one moment be confounded with the statelier figure of Sir Thomas Browne of Norwich, as (so we are told) was lately done in public by a distinguished living statesman.

Nothing can well be more agreeable than the way in which many of these renovated ghosts of half-forgotten story-tellers chatter and chuckle, and flutter their skirts in these pages. Will anybody, we wonder, in the twenty-first century do the same kind service for the novelists of to-day? His Salon will be a crowded one.

It must not be assumed that Richardson's latest biographer and critic is a sworn devotee. He is nothing of the kind, and can bring himself to write quite composedly of the 'imbecilities' of the second part of *Pamela*. He also makes some references to Sterne which, half a century ago, would have made us very angry, but to-day we are content to murmur *Tempus est jam hinc abire me*.

XII

NATHANIEL HAWTHORNE

XII

NATHANIEL HAWTHORNE

Few things mark so relentlessly the flight of Time as it passes unconsciously over our heads as when it is suddenly brought home to old men how long ago it was since they first learnt to love a favourite author. The dates of publication of the two volumes named at the top of the page, separated as they are from each other by nearly half a century, and yet dealing with affection and real distinction with the same subject-matter, serve to remind me that it is now more than seventy years ago since that day in 1856 when, trying hard to keep step with my Father whilst walking down Castle Street in Liverpool, he bent down to me and whispered in my ear, 'Keep your eyes open, for the author of *The Wonder Book* will pass us in a moment.' How hard I stared at Hawthorne as he went by! He was the first author I had ever seen, and though since that happy day I have encountered many of the breed, he still lives in my memory as the handsomest of them all; nor has he lost favour in my sight as an author, though no longer of one wonder-book but of many.

Hawthorne himself has now been dead sixty-four years (May 18, 1864). But how does he stand to-day after all these years, so prolific of story-tellers of divers nationalities and of all shades and descriptions? Has he worn well? What signs does he show of wear and tear? Do the young find him as delightful as did their elders—nay, do those elders themselves, if still alive, when dreamily turning once enchanted pages, altogether succeed in recapturing the ancient charm? To put it bluntly, can we read the *House of the Seven Gables* or the *Blithedale Romance* without skipping?

I should find it easy to answer this last coarsely worded query with an arrogant and blustering 'Certainly we can', yet, remembering that as we are writing of an author unusually free from any taint of humbug, and this, despite the fact that almost from the first Hawthorne possessed a style so perfect in its artistry as to be in itself an incentive to humbug, we are especially behoven to scrape our consciences closely, and to see to it that we say nothing whatever about Hawthorne and his books that is not, at least, truth for us.

Hawthorne heartily disliked many things and many people, but he hated few things more than injudicious praise. When Mr. S. C. Hall praised him injudiciously, Hawthorne begged that he might never be asked to sit next Mr. Hall again. Montaigne tells us that if, after his death, he should chance to hear anyone on earth praising him for a quality he knew he had never possessed, he would return to the world just long enough to give the fellow the lie. Hawthorne resembled Montaigne in many particulars.

So far as Hawthorne's style is concerned, it may safely be pronounced as flawless as ever. How he came by it who can say? That he took great pains is certain. That he burnt thousands and tens of thousands of words we know. His solitary boyhood in the dismal house in Salem, the good old-fashioned books by which he was luckily surrounded and over which he pored, probably prevented his forming early in life bad literary habits, whilst his detached mind, as boy, youth and man, averse from early enthusiasms and make-believe hero-worships, helped him to avoid falling a victim to any of the many bad examples by which he was encompassed. However this mystery of style came about, Hawthorne, after no long time of experimenting, became possessed of a way of writing he never lost—a style it is impossible to parody, for it is at once romantic and realistic, dreamily mystical, yet as sceptical as David Hume's; straightforward and subtle, and managing, as it flows easily along, to create the very temper of mind that is best fitted to enjoy it.

Personally, I have only one criticism, and it is a very minute one, of Hawthorne's style, for it only consists in complaining of his excessive use of the word 'methinks', which is to be found scattered in a too plentiful profusion over all Hawthorne's writings, tales, note-books, even letters. My objection to this word is that it is *too* characteristic, and lets his readers into one of the secrets of his musing style that should have been kept hidden from the profane vulgar.

Has anyone attempted to parody Hawthorne's style of writing? 'Methinks not!'

Leaving, then, as we safely may, Hawthorne in quiet possession of his style, we can proceed to ask how does he stand as a story-teller? Here he has to submit to the fierce competition of many subsequent masters of the craft.

Do we still read Hawthorne for the story or for his wayside comments upon it?

It must be remembered that until 1850, when he was forty-six years old, and published *The Scarlet Letter*, he was only known to a very few people in America as an occasional writer of short stories in American magazines of no great repute; short stories that gained him little notoriety and less cash. I find it almost comical to discover that the old friend of my infancy, *Peter*

NATHANIEL HAWTHORNE

Parley (C. S. Goodrich), whom I pictured as a cheerful old Father Christmas, was in reality the slightly stingy and occasionally impecunious 'publisher' of Hawthorne's struggling efforts.

When these casual contributions to magazines were collected, they made up those *Twice-told Tales* which, though they had no great popularity, made it plain to those who could observe such occurrences that there was someone living in the neighbourhood of Salem, Mass., who knew how to write the English language at least as well as Washington Irving, the then pet American of Albemarle Street.

Hawthorne's first regular novel, *Fanshawe*, was a complete failure, a fate the wise Peter Parley attributed to the fact that its publisher did not know the art of puffery.

Fully to enjoy Hawthorne as a writer of stories, long or short, it is very necessary you should become acquainted with the pit out of which he was dug.

Strangely enough, it is easy to do this, for though Hawthorne was by common consent, from birth to death, a shy, elusive, reticent creature with a bitter rind at the centre of his nature, he belonged to that class of men who no sooner take up a pen and find themselves near an ink-stand, than they become self-communicative. Pinch a page of Hawthorne, and he bleeds. His books, therefore, like Hazlitt's, will be found to contain a buried autobiography. You can follow Hawthorne from place to place all through his life, from Salem to Raymond, from Raymond back again to Salem, from Salem to College, from College back again to Salem, then to Brook Farm in Roxburg with the Transcendentalists—from them to the old Manse, from the old Manse across the Atlantic to Liverpool, from whence he will take you by the hand and force you to accompany him in his excursions through the Old Home, and then to Florence and Rome and the Marble Faun, and finally back to the country of his birth. Too shy ever to speak of himself to his friends, it is his readers who become his intimates.

This habit of his has made the task of his biographers at once easy and exceeding difficult. A biography, or even a portrait-sketch in words, of Hawthorne becomes a Twice-told-Tale, and as any tale told by Hawthorne about himself is pretty sure to be more engaging than the same tale told by somebody else, the biographer finds himself in a quandary; he cannot always be quoting, yet when he ceases to quote, and begins to take up the story on his own account, even a biographer can hardly fail to become conscious of a difference.

Mr. Lloyd Morris has composed 'a Portrait of Hawthorne' for which he deserves both thanks and praise; and written, as it has been, more than sixty years after Hawthorne's death, it gives us pleasant proof how deeply the author of *The Scarlet Letter* and *The House of the Seven Gables* has struck his roots into the beloved soil of his native land.

The portrait Mr. Morris has drawn is an affectionate and sympathetic one, but at the same time it is searching, and is wholly free from that gushing sentimentality which would have disgusted the subject of the picture. Mr. Morris has used the ample material at his disposal with rare judgment, and for those readers who have had the good or bad luck to be born in the present century, and consequently will never think it necessary to read through the lengthy biography prepared by Hawthorne's son Julian, and published in 1885, this book may be warranted to contain all that our young friends need be told about Hawthorne, except what he himself will tell them if they are wise enough to seek the fountain-head.

We have but one fault to find with Mr. Morris, and it is one not far to seek, for it is to be seen on his title-page. Why is Hawthorne described as a rebellious Puritan?

To be a rebel you must at one time or another have been a subject. Hawthorne's early American ancestors were rebels to their lawful Sovereign, and Puritans by religious conviction. Their story-telling descendant was a Republican born and bred and through and through, and as for being a Puritan by religion, he was not one for a single moment.

Never was there a son of Adam less animated, still less dominated, either by the prejudices of a Sectary or the pride of a Churchman. His education was unusually free from the traditions of either Church or Chapel. You cannot fancy Nathaniel being pinioned in a family pew of schismatics, or conducted to a seat in a Church choir. Hawthorne had no occasion to become a rebel; for, like the Apostle Paul, he was born free.

At all times and in all places Hawthorne led the life, the easy-going life, of a sedate and thoughtful Pagan. His habits, seldom otherwise than decorous, bore no traces of what can properly be called Puritan. He was as fond of cards as Charles Lamb, and as good a judge of wine as Cardinal Newman, though, oddly enough, he had not that ear for music usually found associated with a fine palate. Hawthorne must be ranked with those who, like Elia, have 'no ear', for has he not left it on record that he could never distinguish 'Hail, Columbia!' from 'Yankee Doodle'?

Mr. Morris would appear to have come to the conclusion that Hawthorne was in a state of rebellion against a deep-hidden Puritanism in his nature from two facts—the first being Hawthorne's 'austere notions' of sexual morality, and the second the idea or belief that pervades so many of his books and stories, that there is such a thing as sin in the world, and that the existence of this thing has, if one may use such an expression, played the devil with Creation ever since its introduction among the sons of men.

As to the first of these facts, it is very agreeably plain that a strain of personal purity did run through Hawthorne's life, and nowhere is this trait in his character more exquisitely illustrated than in the love-letters he wrote to his wife during their courtship of four years. Of these letters Mr. Morris has, with his usual judgment, made copious use.

Hitherto I have always supposed that personal purity, or chastity as it is sometimes called, is a Christian virtue of universal obligation (however frequently disregarded) upon all, men and women alike, who call themselves Christians; but now it would appear to be a sectarian virtue only appendant to a theory of life styled Puritanical.

As for Hawthorne's doctrine of sin and its consequences entailed upon mankind, a doctrine which he certainly expounds over and over again in his tales (see, for an example, 'Fancy's Show Box' in the *Twice-told Tales*), it can confidently be stated that it has no connection with any doctrine of sin as taught in Geneva, Lambeth, or Rome, or anywhere else throughout what is called

Christendom. It was coined in Hawthorne's own mint, and is half phantasy, half faith.

It is, no doubt, true that though Hawthorne was as unlike a Puritan as Charles Dickens, he was that rare bird, an author with a long pedigree, and one which, though it left his beliefs uncoloured, mightily affected his literary imagination.

Hawthorne's earliest American ancestor was William Hathorne (for the *w* was first inserted by our romantic Nathaniel himself, who thus made the old Puritan stem blossom in the wilderness), who came from pleasant Wiltshire to Massachusetts in 1630, in company with John Winthrop and other fathers and founders of a new country. About the Puritanism of William Hathorne there can be no manner of doubt. He was a Sectary to the backbone and may be taken to be the progenitor of those 'grave, bearded, sable-cloaked and steeple-crowned hatted' figures who tread so heavily, with their misunderstood Bibles in their hands and their sharp swords by their sides, through the pages of Hawthorne's romances, who had not read Scott for nothing.

This William Hathorne 'was soldier, legislator, judge', and a great man and landowner (by virtue of grants) in the neighbourhood of Salem, where for many long years he ruled with a heavy hand that Carlyle might have admired but which exacted a shudder in the breast of one of his descendants. Hathorne was a savage persecutor. Quakers were his aversion. 'He ordered five women of that sect to be stripped to the waist, bound to the tails of carts and lashed by the constable through Salem, Boston and Dedham.'

Nathaniel Hawthorne had no sympathy with separatists of any kind, and would never have insisted upon keeping his hat on his head in any place of worship or court of justice; nor would he, we may be sure, have refused the easy tribute of his knee to any ancient image or symbol; but cruelty based on religion he abhorred. William Hathorne was, consequently, no hero of his, nor was his next ancestor any more to his mind, for when William died in 1681, full of honours, he was succeeded in many of his offices by his son John, an active judge in the colony, and one who never willingly suffered a witch to live. His exceptionally harsh treatment of Rebecca Nurse, who, though twice acquitted by a jury, and protesting to the end her innocence, was hounded to the gallows by Judge Hathorne, who insisted upon a third trial, when he succeeded in securing a verdict of guilty. 'After the sentence had been read, she turned towards Justice Hathorne, and, looking fixedly upon him with old eyes, she solemnly cursed him and his posterity to the last generation.'

Old Rebecca's curse still reverberates in the rafters of *The House of Seven Gables*, and withers drearily through many a dark corner of Hawthorne's romances.

Mr. Justice Hathorne lived ten years after he had done Rebecca to death, and though his local honours accumulated his fortunes declined. Two of his sons died, and he was compelled, owing to unlucky ventures, to borrow money he was unable to repay. When prosperous, he had acquired a wide tract of forest-land in what afterwards became part of the State of Maine, and would have brought untold gold to his descendants, but the title-deeds mysteriously disappeared and the wealth was lost. All this is familiar to Hawthorne's readers.

John Hathorne had several sons who, for the most part, followed the sea, leaving Joseph Hathorne at home to look after the farms and watch the decline of the family fortunes.

'Farmer' Joseph was succeeded by Daniel, a bold mariner, who played a dashing part in the Revolutionary War, earned a fair amount of prize-money, and built himself a house near the Wharfs in Salem, where he died, but not without begetting children, one of whom he called Nathaniel, who in his turn became the father of our Nathaniel, who was born (auspicious day) on the 4th of July, 1804. Nathaniel the elder, who also followed the sea, died abroad in 1808.

Thus it came about that when our author was born his family had been settled in Salem for nearly two centuries, and though luck had of late years deserted them, and newer generations more prosperous than they had grown up in Salem, still the Hathornes held their heads high, brooded over past days, and looked down upon their neighbours.

In 1808 the family in the old wooden house consisted of the widow of Daniel the bold; her daughter Ruth, aged thirty; Nathaniel's mother, the widow of Nathaniel the elder, and her three children: Elizabeth, Nathaniel (aged four), and Louisa.

Hawthorne's mother, though an affectionate and sensible woman, much attached, after her own strange fashion, to her children, led, after her husband's death, a life of East Indian seclusion, passing the whole day in her own room, and only visiting her children in their separate apartments. There were no family meals and nothing that can be called family life. The old grandmother soon died, and what became of Ruth I do not know, except that she died, unmarried, in 1847. Hawthorne's sister Elizabeth, though a girl of great ability and even learning, led almost as lonely a life as her mother. Nathaniel has left it on record that the only thing he was ever really frightened of was Elizabeth's ridicule. His other sister—younger than himself—was of livelier mould.

This was the secluded atmosphere in which Hawthorne grew up. The home, though hardly a home, was happy enough, and in it, barring a serious accident to his foot that crippled him for some time, Nathaniel grew up a vigorous, handsome, robust boy, able to hold his own if occasion arose, and a great reader of Shakespeare, Milton, Bunyan, Thomson (of *The Seasons*), and Rousseau, and, as time went on, of both Scott's and Godwin's novels.

When his tenth year came along, the family migrated from the old house in Salem to still lonelier quarters in Essex County—a tiny settlement called Raymond, on a headland thrust into the Lake Sebago, where the boy, in his own words, 'ran quite wild and would, I doubt not, have willingly run wild until this time, fishing all day long, and on rainy days reading Shakespeare, *The Pilgrim's Progress* and any poetry or light books within my reach'. Hawthorne always looked back upon this wild time with great pleasure and counted it profitable.

He had, however, in his mother's opinion, to be prepared for college, and so, after a time, they all went back to Salem.

After Salem, and some attempts at schooling,

came college. Bowdoin College, in Brunswick, then a ragged village, but, if words have any meaning, pleasantly, even romantically, situated 'on a wide tract of pine forest, where footpaths wound through miles of fragrant shade, and a brook loitered on its way to Androscoggin River'. The college itself seems to have been an easy-going kind of secondary school with a four years' course—with a president at the head of it—and some sort of a degree at the end. A pleasant enough place for a 'general reader' to fleet away his time. Card-playing for stakes and the drinking of wine were no part of the curriculum, and were, indeed, frowned upon by the president. Nevertheless, Nathaniel seems on occasions to have indulged moderately in these unpuritanical pastimes, in a respectable tavern outside the precincts.

There is no need to deplore the absence from Hawthorne's life of the Isis or the Cam. He would probably have got into far more serious scrapes at either Oxford or Cambridge, and certainly would have spent a great deal more of his mother's money. Nor is there much reason to suppose he would have worked any harder anywhere else.

In one respect the college by the Androscoggin supplied the very want English parents in old days used to credit our old universities with supplying, viz. the opportunity of making useful acquaintances—patrons of good livings, and future Prime Ministers and so on. At Bowdoin, by the banks aforesaid, Hawthorne found a future President of the United States, who became his life-long friend, and lived to bestow upon him what was reckoned a fat piece of Uncle Sam's patronage, the Consulship at Liverpool. And besides Mr. Franklin Pierce, was not Longfellow, as popular a bard as ever lightly drew his breath, also a fellow collegian? He was; and though I do not think Hawthorne admired Longfellow as much as he would have liked Longfellow to admire him, the two were always good friends, and it was thought a fine leg-up for Hawthorne when the great Longfellow reviewed favourably one of his books. But the best friend Hawthorne made at college was Horatio Bridge, who always loved him like a brother, and befriended him like the most beneficent of strangers.

In 1825 Hawthorne was back again in the old house at Salem, and there he dwelt for twelve years in the family circle—and twelve dull years they must have been—the *Peter Parley* years of his uneventful, detached life.

And now having conducted Hawthorne to his majority and described his pedigree, we can drop narration, only adding that the most joyous incident in a life not very full of joy was his falling in love with Sophia Peabody, who became his wife. The courtship was, for financial reasons, a long one, for he was not married until 1842.

Previously to this happy event Hawthorne had, on two different occasions, spent some months with the Transcendentalists at Brook Farm, and what happened to him there can be read in the fascinating and ironical pages of *The Blithedale Romance*, from which perusal the reader will be able to form his own opinion as to what Hawthorne really thought of Emerson, Ripley, Thoreau, and that remarkable woman whose memoirs are so well worth reading, Margaret Fuller Ossoli. It is fair to add that these eminent personages entirely failed to recognize themselves in *The Blithedale Romance*.

There is no need here to discuss the general achievements of Hawthorne in Literature.

Some half-dozen of his *Twice-told Tales* and a few *Mosses from an Old Manse* are not likely to be forgotten for many a long day. *The Scarlet Letter* has already lived just as long as I have, and shows fewer signs of impending dissolution. Indeed, its introductory chapter, describing the old Custom House, which is as fine a bit of writing as an Essay of Elia, and no finer bit of writing in its own *genre* has been produced since, may safely be trusted to secure *The Scarlet Letter* house-room in thousands of homes in both hemispheres for a period so indefinite as almost to justify the use of an otherwise absurd term—when applied to a book—immortality. *The House of the Seven Gables* is often reckoned the best of Hawthorne's regularly constructed stories, and though here and there it may grow slumbrous, it is an enchanting volume. Then there is *The Blithedale Romance* and *The Marble Faun,* or (in our English edition) *Transformation*. Finally there is *Our Old Home* (Smith & Elder, 1863. 2 vols.).

On this last-named book, not now so well known as it should be in these days when guide-books to England have become as plentiful as blackberries or anthologies, I should like to be permitted to say a few words.

As already indicated, Hawthorne is, as I read him, a 'bitter-sweet author'. The first stanza in a pretty little poem of Coventry Patmore's called 'The Yew Berry' is, I have always thought, a good description of Hawthorne:—

'I call this idle history the Berry of the Yew,
  Because there is nothing sweeter than its husk of scarlet glue,
  And nothing half so bitter than its dark rind bitten through.'

The state of mind in which, in 1853, Hawthorne approached England for the first time to take up the consulate at Liverpool was a curiously conflicting one, and made up of those 'contending emotions' that were the death of Brian du Bois Guilbert. Love for the old home mingled with a suspicion that he should dislike most of its present inhabitants—a sensitiveness and self-consciousness produced by his secluded life and mode of education, a desperate effort never to allow himself to be carried away by the stirrings of affection for the old place, its sights and sounds, its hedgerows and its ditches, its beasts and birds, so as to shake his faith in the vast superiority of the new home: all these emotions, and others that could be named, inhabited Hawthorne's breast as he took possession of the old consulate office in Liverpool near the Goree Piazza at the corner of Brunswick Street. Liverpool looked its very dirtiest as Hawthorne disembarked. 'Outdoors a brown soupy rain fell incessantly.' Both Nathaniel and his Sophia succumbed to melancholy, feeling themselves aliens and unwelcome.

On the walls of his office hung a large map of the United States, and a similar one of Great Britain. 'On the top of a bookcase stood a fierce and terrible bust of General Jackson, pilloried in a military collar which rose above his ears, and frowning forth immitigably at any Englishman who might happen to cross the threshold. I am afraid, however, that the truculence of the old general's expression was utterly thrown away on this stolid and obdurate race of men; for when they occasionally inquired whom this work of art represented, I was mortified to find that the younger ones had never heard of the battle of New Orleans, and that the elders had either forgotten it altogether, or contrived to misremember, and twist it wrong end foremost into something like an English victory. They have caught from the old Romans this excellent method of keeping the national glory intact, by sweeping all defeats and humiliations clean out of their memory.' (*Our Old Home*, vol. i, p. 3.)

This short extract gives us a little peep into the new Consul's state of mind on entrance into his office.

For my part, I find these two volumes delightful reading. I confess to liking books of travel containing a tinge of underlying dislike in them, and in Hawthorne's case his efforts, so honestly made and so frequently unsuccessful, to fan the flickering flames of his dislike for us, and to choke in the utterance his hearty admiration for so many of our national characteristics, are as exciting to watch as a well-matched game of French and English.

Our Old Home gave great offence in England. There is only one really outrageous passage in the book, and that is the one that describes a fat woman. It is positively Swiftian in its horror and grossness. One of his Liverpool friends, a lady, and a very pretty one, remarkable for the symmetry of her shape, was so justly indignant that she wrote to Hawthorne to tell him that only a cannibal could have written it. However, his English friends forgave him.

In order to get the taste of the fat woman out of my mouth and mind, let me evoke another image culled from the same book. After describing an English hedgerow in terms of rapture, Hawthorne proceeds to describe an English stone wall. 'Or if the roadside has no hedge, the ugliest stone fence (such as in America would keep itself bare and unsympathizing till the end of time) is sure to be covered with the small handiwork of Nature; that careful mother lets nothing go naked there, and if she cannot provide clothing, gives at least embroidery. No sooner is the fence (wall) built than she adopts and adorns it as part of her original plan, treating the hard, uncomely structure as if it had all along been a favourite idea of her own. A little sprig of ivy may be seen creeping up the side of the low wall and clinging fast with its many feet to the rough surface; a tuft of grass roots itself between two of the stones where a pinch or two of wayside dust has been moistened into nutritious soil for it; a small bunch of fern grows in another crevice; a deep, soft, verdant moss spreads itself along the top and over all the available inequalities of the fence; and where nothing else will grow, lichens stick tenaciously to the bare stone and variegate the monotonous grey with hues of yellow and red. Finally, a great deal of shrubbery clusters along the base of the stone wall and takes away the hardness of its outline, and in due time, as the upshot of these apparently aimless or sportive touches, we recognize that the beneficent Creator of all things, working through His handmaiden whom we call Nature, has deigned to mingle a charm of divine gracefulness, even with so earthly an institution as a boundary fence' (vol. i, p. 148).

In Liverpool, Hawthorne made at once many good and lasting friends. Amongst these Henry A. Bright stands out. For some reason or other, Mr. Morris speaks slightingly of Mr. Bright's intellectual stature; I do not know why. Anyhow, Mr. Bright's memory is firmly buttressed, for he wrote a little book called *A Year in a Lancashire Garden*, which, I am assured by those friends of mine who belong to the tenacious and self-satisfied class of botanists, is, in its way, a small masterpiece, and one that is just as likely to achieve literary immortality as *The House of the Seven Gables*. This may or may not be the case, but as I shall not be allowed to give a quotation from Mr. Bright's book, I will pray leave to reprint some descriptive rhymes of his on Hawthorne himself. The whole of this small effort is to be found in Mr. Julian

NATHANIEL HAWTHORNE

Hawthorne's life of his father, but I will make a selection:—

> 'Do you ask me, tell me further
> Of this Consul—of this Hawthorne?
> I would say, he is a sinner,
> Never goes inside a chapel,
> Only sees outsides of chapels,
> Says his prayers without a chapel.
> I would say that he is lazy,
> Very lazy—good for nothing;
> Hardly ever goes to dinner,
> Never goes to balls or soirees—
> Thinks one friend worth twenty friendly.
> Cares for love but not for liking,
> Hardly knows a dozen people,
> Knows old Baucis, old Philemon,
> Knows a beak, and knows a parson,
> Knows a sucking scribbling merchant,
> Hardly knows a soul worth knowing;
> Lazy, good-for-nothing fellow.'

The rhythm of these lines may still be recognizable as that of the once popular *Hiawatha*, a tinkle still pleasing to my ear, and one which is for ever preserved in Dodgson's *Hiawatha's Photographing*—the most amusing of all English parodies.

If Mr. Bright's parody should not be found amusing, it should not be overlooked that Mr. Bright never set up either as a parodist or a poet, but was merely a Liverpool merchant of great credit, the editor of the Glenriddell MSS. of Burns, a lover of good books, old friends, and Lancashire gardens. Hawthorne certainly had no more affectionate friend in England than Mr. Bright, to whom he pays a coyly hidden compliment on page 57 of the first volume of *Our Old Home*.

XIII

'NO CRABB, NO CHRISTMAS'

XIII

'NO CRABB, NO CHRISTMAS'

(A Christmas at Rydal Mount without a visit from Crabb Robinson was thus described by the Wordsworths.)

The Correspondence of Henry Crabb Robinson with the Wordsworth Circle, 1808 to 1866. Edited by Edith I. Morley. Two vols.

IT is startling to be reminded that fifty-seven years have passed away since Dr. Sadler published three stout volumes entitled *Diary, Reminiscences, and Correspondence of Henry Crabb Robinson*, the 'old Crab' of those youngsters Arthur Hugh Clough and Walter Bagehot; and it is strange to be called upon to notice that Dr. Sadler, in his preface, thanks for assistance rendered 'J. Morley, Esquire, Author of *Burke, A Historical Study.*'

The same editor also informed the astonished reader that stout as his three volumes were they did not contain more than one twenty-fifth part of the materials at his disposal. Since 1869 more than half a century is behind us, and it is, in most respects, an entirely new England that is asked to welcome two more volumes dug out of the same

'NO CRABB, NO CHRISTMAS'

pit, and devoted exclusively to Wordsworth and what is called his 'Circle'.

More 'Crab' remains in storage.

The present editor is possibly right in the method here pursued and intended to be pursued in future publications. After Wordsworth, Coleridge will have his turn, and so on till the Robinsonian cupboards in Dr. William's Library are bare.

Those of us who like their reading of Diaries and Reminiscences to be 'mixed reading' so that when we grow aweary of one entourage we can flee into another may demur to this method, but when we think of Miss Morley ruefully surveying those cupboards, it is easy to believe that she had really no choice but to adopt the Roman maxim *Divide et impera!*

So here are two volumes containing, all told, a little over nine hundred pages about Wordsworth, his sister, his wife, his daughter, his sons, his grandsons, and the clerical nephew who wrote his Biography, which some have reckoned the dullest life ever written of a great man except the Life of that famous Judge Lord Hardwicke by somebody of the name of Harris.

These two volumes record the History of a Family told year by year and sometimes month by month, in the language of the hour, and as the things happened, with a frankness, a bluntness that

'NO CRABB, NO CHRISTMAS'

belong to those who had no suspicion that in writing as they did they were doing anything but living out their lives in the secrecy of a sheltered home.

There were times in reading these pages when we felt guilty of an almost indecent intrusion upon the private sorrows of proud and reserved spirits. We are ready enough to believe that most family records extending over three generations, when reported truthfully, bluntly, and untinged by sloppy sentiment or sickly religiosity, cannot but be painful reading; yet over this Vale of Grasmere there hung clouds so black and sorrows so permanent as to make the sustained study of these volumes more than usually melancholy.

All true Wordsworthians, and many who have never been guilty of idolatry at that shrine, love the very name of the poet's sister—the 'dear, dear sister', the eternal nymph of Tintern Abbey, the wildest creature that ever lived, and the most powerful external human influence her brother ever felt. How can we do else but cry as we trace her history in the first of these volumes? Down to the end of 1831, she is Robinson's chief correspondent, and her letters reveal her careless charm. Rydal Mount without Dorothy, how could it endure? Then about the date just mentioned she drops out; and though living at Rydal Mount for

'NO CRABB, NO CHRISTMAS'

five years after her brother's death in 1850, she only figures in the family correspondence as 'my poor sister', or, more painful still, as 'dear old Auntie'. Her illness was mental, and sometimes it is described too bluntly. To think of such a spirit so 'o'erthrown' is terrible.

De Quincey, who, to do the spiteful but subtle creature justice, loved Dorothy, has made us all laugh over Wordsworth's inability to pick up a lady's glove, or to hand her out or even into her carriage, but until his own death and for twenty years of his sister's illness he never forgot to catch in her voice the language of his former heart, or to read his former pleasures in the 'shooting lights' of her wild eyes. Wordsworth all these long years never wished her to die, however much others of a younger generation might have thought it would have been a merciful relief. He could not endure the thought of such a loss. Even the kind-hearted Crabb thought this was odd. We find it hard to forgive Edward Quillinan (Wordsworth's son-in-law) his reference to Dorothy: 'Miss W. was in a deplorable way for her brother's departure from home, *for he, you know, spoils her, poor thing* (vol. ii, p. 674).

After this melancholy and prolonged occultation of Dorothy, the death of his daughter (Dora Quillinan) in July, 1847, broke the heart of the tough old poet. It dissolved him into tears, and

'NO CRABB, NO CHRISTMAS'

when left alone he had long fits of weeping. A Wordsworth in floods of tears is not a familiar figure to his admirers. His mind and will remained as strong as ever, for there was little room for mere sentiment in his self-centred nature, but he found it wellnigh impossible to live without sight of her. Robinson reports to Miss Fenwick, one of Wordsworth's dearest friends and neighbours, whom he was wont to greet each morning with 'a smacking kiss', how when he (Crabb) was lamenting to old James Dixon, the faithful family servant, his master's inability 'to submit to the will of Providence', James replied: 'Ah! sir, so I took the liberty of saying to master, but he said, "Oh! but she was such a bright creature"; and when I answered, "But, sir, don't you think she is brighter now than ever she was?" then master burst into a flood of tears.' Wordsworth's religion was an immense support to him, but gave him little comfort.

The tragedies connected with the names of S. T. C., and his son Hartley, in whom Wordsworth had taken great delight, which lives in immortal verse as 'a blessed vision', and with the latter days of Southey were, of course, less poignant than the two we have mentioned, for Wordsworth's sympathy with the elder Coleridge was always 'imperfect', whilst with Southey he had none at all; but they all combined to

'NO CRABB, NO CHRISTMAS'

cast a deep shadow over the Vale and its tiny Churchyard.

The frequently recurring names of Charles and Mary Lamb bestow a benediction over these volumes. Wordsworth's love for them was deep and enduring.

XIV

THOMAS LOVE PEACOCK

XIV

THOMAS LOVE PEACOCK
(1785–1866) OR

THE GROWTH OF THE PAVONIAN LEGEND

WE have always counted it one of the happiest chances of our literary life when, one dusky November afternoon in 1869, we captured, for the easy equivalent of eighteenpence, in Messrs. Reeves and Turner's second-hand bookshop, then at the west end of Fleet Street, nearly opposite old Temple Bar and close by Groom's coffee-house, where junior members of the legal profession were accustomed to take their milder kinds of refreshment, and Carter's hairdressing establishment, the Fifty-seventh volume of Bentley's 'Standard Novels', containing *Headlong Hall*, *Nightmare Abbey*, *Maid Marian*, and *Crotchet Castle*, with a wonderful Preface by their then almost unknown author, dated March, 1837.

We must have casually heard of Peacock before that happy hour, for otherwise we might have let the chance go by, but as it was:—

'With this, one glance at the letter'd back of which
And "Stall", cried I, a lira made it mine.'

THOMAS LOVE PEACOCK

Shortly after 1869, with a whetted appetite, I had no great difficulty in purchasing, though at the enhanced price of three shillings, Peacock's last novel, *Gryll Grange*, published in 1861; and after that, for six shillings and sixpence, an excellent edition of his collected works, in three volumes, with a short preface, somewhat coolly composed by Lord Houghton, and also containing a short but admirable biography of her grandfather by Miss Edith Nicolls (Bentley, 1875).

It was our good fortune to have had a slight acquaintance in old days at Blackheath with Miss Nicolls, who was the only child of a gallant lieutenant of the Navy, who lost his life whilst attempting to save that of a brother seaman. Miss Nicolls's mother was Peacock's eldest daughter, who died in 1861, having married, for the second time, George Meredith. Miss Nicolls was, as were all his grandchildren, greatly attached to Peacock, though, as her short biography shows, fully alive to his many out-of-the-way characteristics.

In this collected edition of 1875, *Melincourt* makes a new appearance after the date of its first publication in 1817; also the early poetry and the Shelley papers. After 1875 there have been various editions, and, slowly but surely, Peacock has become, after his own fashion, a popular author, and now lies embalmed, but we trust not buried, in the numerous handsome volumes of the

'Holleford' edition (Constable). But for us he must always remain as he was in 1869, a discovery of our own.

In the May term at Cambridge in 1870, and for the first time, I composed an article and took Peacock as my subject, and after many doubts dispatched it to the magazine I thought most likely to receive it kindly—the *Temple Bar Magazine*. It was posted in Petty Cury (I can vouch for that), but was never seen or heard of again. And now, after nearly sixty years, I find myself, by request, scribbling on the same theme. I am, happily, in no danger of repeating myself. Those sixty years, though they have made no difference in the pleasure still taken in the eighteenpenny volume, which lies before me as I write, have altered the point of view and destroyed the sense of ownership once felt.

In 1870 we were puffed up, however mistakenly, in the boastful spirit of a pioneer, and felt as if no one else had ever appreciated *Crotchet Castle*, and as if *Maid Marian* was only known on the stage by its lyrics. Now, it would be impossible even for a boy of twenty to cherish such an illusion. Everybody now knows, or pretends to know, all Peacock's novels, and some of his poetry. Of course, we are glad it should be so.

The character behind the books has undergone no change. We cannot bring ourselves to believe that Peacock belonged to that large class of authors who, as Mr. Arnold Bennett so persistently and so usefully keeps reminding us, write for money, finding it easier in that way to support themselves and their families than it would be in any other way. Peacock, though poor enough to start with, obtained in 1819 a clerkship in the East India Office, after an examination for which he was only allowed six months' preparation, and there he remained hard at work until 1856, when he retired on a pension—to give the exact figures, of £1,333 6s. 8d.—a sum quite sufficient in those days to keep the wolf from his door without driving him to the necessity (to use the late Lord Young's savage sarcasm) of trying to do so by the expedient of reading his own poetry to the wolf. But why do authors who have made their pile go on writing just as if they needed to do so? Shakespeare, it is true, left off writing, but others go on. It must be in obedience to a primordial instinct.

Peacock's prejudices were multiform, manifold, and, so at least we thought in 1869, meritorious. Amongst his hatreds were Bob Southey, Lord Brougham, the Edinburgh Reviewers, the Political Economists, the Metaphysicians, and (though here we parted company with him) the whole school of romantic poets and novelists, even going so far as to call *The Ancient Mariner* an 'irresistibly comic ballad'. Lord Houghton discovered in Peacock 'an element of unreasoning animosity', and that he was, first and foremost, a satirist need not be denied; but at this distance of time as there is more comicality than savagery in his satire it is easy to forgive him, particularly when there is now so little satire to be had in the bookshops.

If room can be found for them, some specimens of Peacock's wares should be given, and they shall be selected from the least well-known of his novels, *Melincourt,* whose hero, the dumb Sir Orang Houtang, who played on the flute and was returned to Parliament as a Member for Old Sarum, was rather too much for the novel readers of 1817. Here is an extract on *Taste*:—

'*The Hon. Mrs. Pinmoney.*—Tastes—they depend on the fashion. There is always a fashionable taste, a taste for driving the mail, a taste for acting Hamlet, a taste for philosophical lectures, a taste for the marvellous, a taste for the grim, a taste for banditti, a taste for ghosts, a taste for Italian singers and French dancers, and German whiskers and tragedies, a taste for enjoying the country in November, and wintering in London during the dog-days, a taste for picturesque tours, a taste for taste itself, or for Essays on Taste; but no gentleman would be so rash as to have a taste of his own, or his last winter's taste, or any taste, my love, but the fashionable taste.'

The next and last extract shall be in another

vein, and describes a hot dispute between Mr. Feathernest (Bob Southey) and Mr. Derrydown over Chapman's *Homer* and Jeremy Taylor's *Holy Living*:

'Mr. Derrydown maintaining that the ballad metre which Chapman had so judiciously chosen rendered his volume the most divine poem in the world; Mr. Feathernest asserting that Chapman's verses were mere doggerel, which vile aspersion Mr. Derrydown revenged by depreciating Mr. Feathernest's favourite Jeremy. Mr. Feathernest said he could expect no better judgment from a man who was mad enough to prefer *Chevy Chase* to *Paradise Lost*, and Mr. Derrydown retorted that it was idle to expect either taste or judgment from a man who had thought fit to unite in himself two characters so anomalous as a poet and a critic, in which duplex capacity he had at first deluged the world with torrents of execrable verse, and then written anonymous criticisms to prove them divine. "Do you think, sir," he continued, "that it is possible for the same man to be both Homer and Aristotle? No, sir, but it is very possible to be both Dennis and Colley Cibber, as in the melancholy example before me".'

The dispute did not end here, but the quotation must.

The Oxford University Press have just added to their series of the 'World's Classics' *Headlong Hall and Nightmare Abbey* (2s.); a very pretty little book indeed.

XV

HICKEY
(1749–1830)

XV

HICKEY
(1749–1830)

MEMOIRS OF WILLIAM HICKEY
Vol. I, 1913
Vol. II, 1918
Vol. III, 1923
Vol. IV, 1925
(Hurst and Blackett)

(*These reviews were written at different dates*)

I

THE PEDIGREE OF MANUSCRIPTS

EDITORS of manuscripts, whether of Dramas destined for Immortality, like those usually attributed to Shakespeare or of Epics like those passing under the name of Ossian, or merely manuscripts like those which have given rise to these reflections, detailing the adventures of lively blackguards or sots, or of ladies without reputation, cannot be too careful to supply the best evidence procurable of the authenticity of the documents they take upon themselves to publish; and the easiest and most natural way of doing this is by rendering a full, true, and particular account, out of whose custody they got the manuscripts they print.

Had editors always been mindful of this, their first and their chief duty, the world would now be a very different place. Only to think of the Preface of the two Actors to the First Folio of 1623 is to be full of sorrow. If those editors had thought fit to tell us where they got their improved readings of the previously published plays, and their versions of the plays printed for the first time in 1623, how much worry, boredom, vain speculation, backbitings, malice, and downright hatred would have been prevented. But, like our first parents, they disregarded their chief duty, and so, though it may not be alleged against them that they first brought death into the world, it can truthfully be said that their foolish reticence has enormously increased the measure of our woe.

Consider, even though it may be only for a moment, the hard fate of Ossian (? James Macpherson), the favourite poet of Goethe and Napoleon, the Fountain of Romance at which Burns and Wordsworth drank their early draughts of inspiration. Why is Ossian (or Macpherson) docked of his poetic sizings, denied his place among bards, and kept out of that purgatory of poets, our popular and numerous anthologies? The answer is easy—the pedigree of his papers. Where are the Ossian manuscripts?

HICKEY

When, towards the end of 1913, the first volume of the Memoirs of William Hickey took the town, and not surprisingly—for who is not ready to hail almost uproariously the appearance of a brand-new blackguard found to possess the gift too rarely bestowed upon blackguards of being agreeable in print?—it could not fail to be observed by the most careless reader that the editor told us nothing about the manuscript, save that it covers many hundreds of closely written folio pages, with only two or three corrections (here resembling Shakespeare's), and presenting the appearance of being a clean copy made from a rough draft. Now, to speak bluntly, this is not enough, and it could not but follow from this strange reticence that the cautious reader, anxious not to be fooled by another De Foe, was from the very first fretted by doubt which, as is the way with doubts, grew and grew upon him as he continued to read. Faked memoirs are to the reader what faked title-pages are to the collector of old books, horrid possibilities, for both abound. Was this scandalous but ever-cheerful Hickey a reality, and are these Memoirs genuine? I laid down the first volume but half convinced.

Five years pass by—horrible years in the world's history—and now appears a second volume, and a third is promised. I turned at once to the new preface to see whether the editor—like the world, five years older—had anything more to tell us about the pedigree of his papers. He had—a little —not much. It now appears that the Hickey manuscript was first shown to 'its present owner' in 1880 by a 'very old friend', into whose possession it came on the death of 'a relative' in or about the year 1865. How this relative got hold of it is not known, though it is suggested that he (or she) might have received it from Hickey himself, the date of whose death has not yet been told us.

'Obstinate questionings' are not got rid of after this fashion; and when a doubt engendered in the breast five years ago has lain there ever since, to disperse it requires more vigorous massage than can be administered by very old friends and relatives unnamed.

Receiving no help from the editor, I set about the business myself, and tried to discover whether there exists anywhere any evidence, however slight, outside and beyond this vagrant, 'clean copy of a rough draft', that such a man as William Hickey, who alleges himself to have been born in 1749, ever existed at all. Very little evidence would, I knew, satisfy me.

The William Hickey of the manuscript tells us that he was the seventh child and the third son of a well-known, highly respected, and, if William were indeed his son, deeply to be pitied London attorney, who figures so pleasantly in Goldsmith's *Retaliation*:—

> 'Here Hickey reclines a most blunt, pleasant creature,'

etc.

Early annotators of these immortal lines have told us that Goldsmith's Hickey was otherwise known as 'Honest Tom Hickey', though if we are to believe the Memoirs his name was Joseph, but as it appears Joseph had a brother Tom, nothing ought to be made of this discrepancy. Annotators are often wrong. Still, amongst the passages in the Memoirs that fed my initial doubt was the one which occurs on page 308 of the first volume, where a reference is dragged in to Goldsmith's famous poem so inaccurate as to make anybody acquainted with the genesis of the poem not a little uncomfortable.

To cut the matter short, I have happened upon something which at all events convinces me that there was once upon a time a man called William Hickey, a son of Goldsmith's Hickey, and that the Memoirs now in course of publication are entitled to just so much credence as wary folk are in the habit of bestowing upon the authenticated writing of lively and unprincipled liars. I have not room for all my reasons for this conclusion, but I will give one.

The Hickey of these Memoirs tells us, and he is

good at dates, that he was an attorney in Calcutta from November, 1777, to April, 1779, and that during this period he was selected from the Corps of Attorneys to act for Mr. Grand in the famous action for damages brought by that gentleman against Sir Philip Francis for undue familiarity with Madame Grand, afterwards the wife of Talleyrand, the Princess Benevento, and the heroine of so many humorous, if ill-natured, stories to be found in the gay records of French anecdotage. Hickey goes on to tell us how he had to decline this profitable bit of business, 'not from any particular attachment to Francis, but from motives of delicacy towards my respected friend Mr. Burke, who had introduced me to him' (vol. ii, p. 158); but, though thus shorn of his costs, he continued to follow the case, as indeed did every white face in Calcutta, with the keenest interest. The Court which tried the issue consisted of Sir Elijah Impey, who hated Francis almost as fiercely as Francis deserved to be hated; Mr. Justice Hyde, who on this point, at all events, was entirely of the same mind with his chief; and Mr. Justice Chambers, who was much attached to Francis, and hated Impey and Hyde. Such a tribunal in such a case was perhaps bound to differ. Anyhow differ they did; Impey and Hyde deciding that Francis was guilty and mulcting him with damages to the tune of 50,000 rupees, whilst Chambers had no difficulty whatever in declaring that no evidence worthy of the name had been produced against his friend Francis. Such are the instruments of human justice!

Hickey, who represents himself as being present at the trial, repeats, as if he had heard it, a time-honoured story, since discredited—viz. how when Impey assessed the damages at 50,000 rupees, his brother Hyde, in his eagerness to make Francis smart, in a low but audible voice murmured, 'Siccas'. On which the Chief Justice added, 'Aye, siccas, Brother Hyde.' Whereupon, says Hickey, a roar of mirth convulsed the court, at which Sir Elijah was greatly offended (vol. ii, p. 160). Is it necessary to add that 'sicca' rupees were of the highest denomination?

Now until the publication of this second volume this tale has never been traced farther back than 1822, when it appeared in a book of small value, *Personal Recollections*, by John Nicholls, M.P. The legal mind, fond as it is of a joke and always indifferent as to its quality, has never taken kindly to this anecdote, pointing out that, as the plaintiff's claim for damages was laid in 'sicca' rupees, there was really no occasion for Brother Hyde's interruption, a criticism which, though just, is not destructive, nor indeed likely to convince any frequenter of Courts of Justice that the irrelevant interruption was not in fact made.

If Hickey really existed and these Memoirs are genuine, this old story of the 'siccas' may now be said to have been set once more upon its rickety legs.

But why, it may be asked, have I come to believe in Hickey, and what can an action of crim.-con. brought against Sir Philip Francis in Calcutta in the year 1778 have to do with the genuineness of these Memoirs? Only this: on being reminded by Hickey in his second volume of this bit of Calcutta scandal I took down one of the best books ever written about old Calcutta days, called *Echoes from Old Calcutta*, the work of a man devoted to his subject and beloved by his friends, Dr. Busteed, the second edition of which bears date 1888. In this book there is a full and most entertaining account of the crim.-con. case and of the subsequent adventures in England and in France of the frail creature who, whatever may be said and proved against her, was good enough and chaste enough to be the wife of Talleyrand!

It was whilst re-reading Dr. Busteed my eye suddenly encountered in a note at the foot of page 199 the name of William (or at least W.) Hickey, a Calcutta attorney. I gave a start like Robinson Crusoe's, and when I read on and found the name vouched for in a Report of a Select Committee of the House of Commons, printed at the public expense in 1782, and, what

HICKEY

is more, a quotation from this now identified Hickey in language so animated that I found it familiar, the bundle of my doubts, like Christian's heavy burden, fell off my back and vanished for ever.

Thus relieved of this weight, I at once began, 'glad and lightsome', to find other confirmations, with which, happily, there is no need to trouble anyone, though the serious student may be recommended to compare the life of that blustering rogue, Commodore Johnston, in the *Dictionary of National Biography*, with Hickey's highly humorous account of the Commodore's marriage with the shrew, Kate Dee, which took place in Lisbon in 1782 (see vol. ii, p. 380).

As for the Memoirs themselves, now that we are quit of our doubts, they may safely be pronounced to possess merits which, considering the class to which they belong, are unusually great.

This Calcutta attorney was, in a vulgar phrase, a 'bad egg' from the beginning. As a boy at school, he was depraved; as a clerk in his father's most respectable office, a thief of peculiar meanness, for he put into his own pocket the guineas that were intended to purchase the forensic energies of Thurlow and Dunning; as a man, he was a spendthrift and a fop, as well as a scandalous ill-liver; yet, as sometimes happened, he carried about with him traces of better things. His heart, though certainly not in the right place, nor anywhere near it, readily responded to some of the claims of humanity. He was neither a coward nor a hypocrite, unless it be hypocrisy to try to make yourself out a bigger blackguard than perhaps you are.

It is unfortunate that these Memoirs throw no sidelights upon Hickey's character. There is no independent testimony, no letters either written by or, better still, addressed to him. We know nothing about him except what he tells us himself, and his word is wellnigh worthless.

To quote from his lively pages is hardly worth while, for Hickey has neither a character to maintain nor a word to pass. Hickey assures us that Thurlow was his 'fast friend', and that the future Lord Chancellor once introduced him to a general company after this engaging fashion: 'This is a wicked dog, who does with me what he likes—a son of Jo. Hickey!'

No better judge of wickedness was to be found than Thurlow, who was probably the wickedest dog that ever soiled the Woolsack, and if he really pronounced this verdict it would be valuable and conclusive. But did Thurlow ever say anything of the sort? The worst of being a liar is that nobody believes a word you say.

One thing, and one thing alone, is agreeably certain, and that is to have been the son of 'Jo.

Hickey' was, *circa* 1770–1785, a passport round the world. The use made of this passport in Jamaica, Calcutta, Lisbon, and elsewhere is written at large over these Memoirs; and though many of their pages are unedifying, and some even disgusting, cannot the same remark be made of far more celebrated volumes than *Hickey's Memoirs* are ever likely to be? One reader at all events awaits with pleasurable expectations the third volume.

II

A Voyage to India

What, is has been often asked, makes the magical difference between a good book and a bad one? This searching question may, and possibly does, admit of an answer, but as its investigation would have to be conducted by way of example, it could not fail to give dire offence in certain sensitive quarters. It is not a question of mere preference of one book over another, or one author over another, as, for example, in the dispute over Gray and Collins, but of a final and damnatory judgment; for if you come to the conclusion that a book is a bad one, what is that but to say that it has no right to exist, as Mr. Arnold was once led to affirm of somebody's translation of the *Iliad*.

HICKEY

To deny the right of existence must always be a serious matter, and in these days of over-production, when books, or semblances of books, appear monthly in their thousands, heralded and trumpeted by the loud cries of their perspiring publishers, all vouching their own wares as veritable masterpieces, and declaring beforehand that if, for example, any particular volume assumes the shape of a memoir, that it will not only brook, but challenge a comparison with Pepys or Evelyn; in these days, we repeat, it would be a dangerous thing to deny to any book the right to exist. Happily, about Hickey there can be no doubt. If Hickey is not a good book may 'The Bodleian' perish!

The first volume of these Memoirs (1749–1775) appeared in 1913, eleven years ago, and left hundreds of readers hungry and athirst for their completion. A good book has no need to hurry. Five years passed before the second volume (1775–1782) made its appearance, and now in 1923 the third volume comes to hand, taking us down to 1790, but still leaving us quite uninformed as to what the ultimate fate of the memorialist is to be. At this moment we do not know when Hickey died, nor where, nor how. As he was born in Pall Mall in 1749, the seventh and most graceless son of that 'blunt and pleasant creature' the Hickey of Goldsmith's *Retaliation*, he can hardly be alive to-day; but though he must be dead by this time, many an old man, who is still alive, may be found praying to live long enough to see the publication of that fourth volume, which we are assured by the somewhat too reticent editor will conduct us to Hickey's tomb, and thus bring to a natural end the most varied and interesting, and in their way the most valuable, Memoirs that have appeared since we know not when.

Owing to the fact that the editor in his short note to the first volume said nothing about how he came into possession of the original manuscript of these Memoirs, and in his note to the second volume only told us that in 1880 the original document was first shown 'to the present owner by an old friend who had received it, with other effects, on the death of a relative some fifteen years before that date', it was not unnatural that doubts should have arisen in the minds of some readers as to whether such a man as William Hickey ever existed. We hate being hoaxed. Was not the elder Pitt taken in by one of Defoe's masterpieces in the art of deception? Sham memoirs are to the judicious reader what title-pages in facsimile are to the collector of rare books—bugbears and horrors of the bedchamber. These nightmare doubts are now happily dissipated. The great interest the two volumes excited, not only at home, but in Jamaica, India, the Cape and other places beyond the seas speedily raised up a cloud of witnesses to prove that such a vagabond as Hickey had undoubtedly existed. Letters arrived, retailing old family traditions, as to the doings of Hickey and his boon companion, Robert Pott, that placed this pleasing fact beyond the pale of controversy. We wish we could give some of them, but must be content with one weighty bit of evidence. In the famous lists of weights of men about town, still preserved in the old wine-shop of Messrs. Berry, in St. James's Street, appear, under the date of November 17, 1808, the two following entries:—

> Mr. Hickey, $11\frac{1}{2}$ in boots.
> Mr. Burke, $12 \cdot 5\frac{1}{2}$ in boots.

This Mr. Burke is not, of course, the celebrated Edmund, but his nephew. A wise legal maxim bids us remember that witnesses should be weighed and not counted, so that we are glad to be able to produce Hickey as a witness for (or against) himself, to the extent of eleven and a half stone 'in his boots'.

But now we must take up the thread of Hickey's Memoirs, if, indeed, such a homely, housewifely word as 'thread' can be applied, with any degree of propriety, to so undomestic a narrative.

This third volume begins most magnificently. Seldom, if ever, has it fallen to our happy lot to read such a story of a journey round the Cape in the old days of sailing-ships. We should dearly love to have Mr. Conrad's opinion of it. It must be read, line by line, to do it any sort of justice; for it is detailed, yet simple, occasionally truly—almost nobly—eloquent, and at all times heart-stirring. The voyage began from Lisbon in June, 1782, on board a Portuguese vessel manned with Portuguese sailors, with an heroic boatswain of superhuman energy and courage. Madeira was reached on June 27th, where for a few days the travellers, soon to be tempest-tossed, went ashore and amused themselves after the fashion in which Hickey excelled. He had for his companions *du voyage* the lovely and charming Charlotte, *née* Barry, whom he had with great gallantry and courage rescued from the barbarous treatment of that fashionable blackguard, Captain Henry Mordaunt, of whom we have already read too much in the second volume, and her faithful servant Harriet, who, shortly after leaving the Funchal Roads, died and was buried at sea.

After leaving Madeira, on July 1st, bound for India, during the months of August and September, the ship went through many experiences, encountering bad weather and losing her reckonings. October was still worse, and November worst of all.

The misfortunes of Charlotte, left without her

faithful maid, are indescribable, save in detail, but she bore them all with such patient endurance and sweetness as to win the utmost sympathy from everyone on board. Hickey's conduct to her was not only beyond reproach but positively angelic. They were often without a cabin to shelter, or food or drink to sustain them. Many of the crew were swept overboard. On November 17th they barely escaped sinking with the ship, now almost a wreck. Prayers, much to Hickey's amazement, were given up, even by the pious Portuguese, and it was in a terrible plight that at last, on November 30, 1782, they sighted Ceylon, but only to discern the French flag floating in the harbour of Trincolmalay, and to learn that it had been taken by the enemy.

On reaching Trincolmalay they were, at first, treated as a possible 'prize', for though the *Rayna de Portugal* flew the Portuguese flag and was manned by a Portuguese crew, the cargo was suspected to be 'enemies' goods', and in point of fact the ship was ultimately condemned and the cargo confiscated by the French Admiralty Court. Hickey, who always expected to be received wherever he went, war or no war, with open arms and invited ashore to get drunk, got into a great rage, but his overtures, friendly or furious, were rebuffed, until in a happy moment for him and his Charlotte the great French Admiral, De

Suffren, appeared on the scene, and all was at once changed. It is nothing short of glorious to witness the revivification of this great Admiral and veritable sea-dog, as much like an Englishman as Nelson was like a Frenchman, in the vigorous pages of Hickey. The two men took to each other from the first, and the beautiful Charlotte was loaded with very necessary presents, the gifts of the gallant sailor, and the fact, in no way disguised, that they consisted of loot taken from her country-women, did not in the least interfere with Charlotte's satisfaction in being thus reclothed and redecorated from head to foot.

Here is Hickey's account of his first sight of the famous Frenchman:—

'In appearance he looked more like a little, fat, vulgar, English butcher than a Frenchman of consequence, in height about five feet five inches, very corpulent, scarcely any hair upon the crown of his head, the sides and back tolerably thick. Although quite grey, he wore neither powder nor pomatum, nor any curl, having a short cue of three or four inches, tied with a piece of old spun-yarn. He was in slippers— a pair of old shoes, the straps being cut off; blue cloth breeches unbuttoned at the knees, cotton, or thread stockings (none of the cleanest) hanging about his legs, no waistcoat, or cravat, a coarse linen shirt entirely wet with perspiration, open at the neck, the sleeves being rolled up above his elbows, as if just going to wash his hands and arms. . . . I afterwards ascertained that he always appeared as above described during the morning.'

What a portrait! More like Commodore Trunnion in *Peregrine Pickle* than Admiral Nelson! But for all his corpulence, this golden-hearted mariner could pull himself alongside a ship with the nippiest of 'middies'. This is the same Admiral Suffren whose sudden death in Paris, in 1788, occasioned a fierce controversy as to whether he died in a duel or in a fit of apoplexy. (See Jals's *Dictionnaire Critique* under name *le Bailli de Suffren*.)

The long conversations between Hickey and this famous Vice-Admiral of France, and the subsequent ones between Hickey and the English Admiral, Sir Edward Hughes, are of historical value, and are not likely to escape the attention of naval historians on both sides of the Channel. Both Admirals greatly appreciated each other; and if we cannot help preferring the Frenchman, it is perhaps because the Englishman left a fortune of £400,000 behind him to be squandered by a stepson. (See *D.N.B.*, vol. xxviii, p. 172.)

But here we must stop. Space has not yet been abolished. For some reasons we cannot regret having to leave Hickey at sea, for on dry land he becomes 'wet', losing his virtues and only retaining his native charm. After being detained at Madras in trying circumstances, and where he witnessed the First Burial of Sir Eyre Coote, he eventually reached Calcutta on June 30, 1783. In Calcutta Hickey, after a preliminary difficulty with his old enemy, Sir Elijah Impey, who during Hickey's absence had caused his name to be struck off the Roll of Attorneys, resumed his legal practice and also too many of his bad habits. As long as Charlotte was by his side Hickey's life was reputable enough; but when she died, as she did on Christmas Day, six months after her arrival in Calcutta, where, as 'Mrs. Hickey', she was held in high esteem, he became a scandalous ill-liver, though quick in his business, and, as ever, agreeable in his manners.

The tales he tells of 'Old Calcutta' are animated, amusing and instructive, and he makes all his scandals credible. We await with eager expectation the fourth volume.

III

Hickey No More

It is strange to recall that more than twelve blood-stained years have gone by since the first volume of these amazing Memoirs of a man wholly forgotten, and about whose very existence grave doubts were at first entertained, made its appearance. No pains were taken either by editor or publisher to dissipate these doubts, and even now, though we are as certain of Hickey having once existed as we are of anything in this spectacular world, we have still no assurance beyond the actuarial tables of our insurance companies, and the general beliefs of mankind that he is not, at this moment, alive at the age of 177. The manuscript of the Memoirs, all in Hickey's clear hand-writing, ends abruptly in 1809, after his final melancholy return to England, and it is clear from the text that it was completed in 1813 or the next year:—

'The date of his death is uncertain, but he is believed to have been the William Hickey whose name is given in the following entry in the old Register of burials in St. Pancras Churchyard.

> 'Name—William Hickey.
> Abode—Little King Street.
> When buried—31st May, 1830.
> Age—70 years.'

In 1830 the William Hickey of the Memoirs was eighty years of age, but as the name of Hickey is not recorded in the rate-books of the parish as a householder, the death above recorded probably occurred in lodgings; and as our Hickey had survived not only his parents, but his brothers and sisters, and most, if not all, his friends, the discrepancy in age is not important. It would seem to have been a lonely ending for so vivacious and companionable a man. No will has been traced, nor the grant of Letters of Administration. The editor suggests that during these twenty years he lived on his capital; if so, we hope from the bottom of our hearts it lasted long enough to supply the solitary old man's needs.

One disadvantage of this publication at considerable. intervals of time is that some readers may be led to read these Memoirs backwards, which would be a prodigious mistake. Hickey must be studied *ab ovo*. To describe Hickey as ever having become a brand snatched from the burning would be ludicrous, but when we remember the first volume, and that at the age of fourteen he was as depraved a little rascal as ever seemed predestined to bring the grey hairs of a respectable London solicitor in sorrow to the grave, it must be cheerfully admitted that as life went on Hickey slowly but steadily improved. His father could never quite be reconciled, but his twin-sisters continued to love him and to correspond with him; and even his father, whose memory is kept alive in twelve lines of Goldsmith's, went on living and spending the whole of his income until 1794.

HICKEY

In this last volume Hickey, in feeling terms, records his father's death:—

'Thus without a pang did my lamented parent leave the world. Subsequent letters which I received from my sisters stated that after death his countenance was as serene and unchanged as if in a gentle slumber. Never did there exist a fonder or more affectionate father than he was to me—in fact he had always been too partially so. Too true it is, that throughout my life, but especially in the early part of it, I made a most ungracious return for all his indulgent kindnesses by thwarting, and counter-acting all his plans for my future well-doing in life. Having always lived expensively, and up to the full amount of his income, he left scarce any property behind him.' (In fact, £600.)

The reader who wisely begins at the beginning will be able to judge for himself how far this amiable extract is a sufficient *amende* for the sheer infamy of the son's behaviour 'in the early part' of his life. But to moralize over the author of these Memoirs would be ridiculous. We may be sure that a delighted posterity will let Hickey off far too easily, as we always do our deceased benefactors. That he put into his own pocket money entrusted to him to pay the fees of Thurlow and Dunning and spent it in debauchery is not, in 1926, an offence to wax eloquent over. How do we know how Thurlow and Dunning, both grossly overpaid men, would have spent the money if it had ever reached them? Still, roguery is roguery, and there was honour among articled clerks, even in the eighteenth century.

Now that we have these four volumes safe in our clutches it is time we should proclaim their startling merits and enduring excellence. They came to us, like Old Age Pensions, bolts from the blue, and have held us in their grip ever since, and we may be sure that those who come after us will never let go their hold upon Hickey. Not only are these volumes good reading from beginning to end, glancing and tripping along; not only are they full of shipwrecks, murders and suicides; of marvellous changes in the fortunes of men and women; of anecdotes of heroes, like the Duke of Wellington in his early days, and of quasi-heroes like the duke's brother, the vainest even of marquesses, but this last volume of all drips with the blood of mutiny and massacres and of horrible revenges; and yet amidst these horrors you may suddenly light upon the enchanted name of Landor's Rose Aylmer, and reconsecrate a night of sighs over her early death in India. But these episodical charms should not conceal the fact that all through Hickey there runs a vein of History of our East Indian Empire in the days of John Company and Leadenhall Street that nowhere else is to be struck upon. It is not a vein that can be opened with more than a very small mixture of pride and pleasure, but it flows freely enough.

There are few more 'informing' books than Hickey's Memoirs.

The romance of Hickey's life disappeared in December, 1783, with the death of his beloved Charlotte Barry, and his worst debauchery ended with Tom Pott. He gradually became, if not always sober, occasionally serious. His life, like that of most Anglo-Indians of the period, was not fit for the inspection of the Church Missionary Society, which indeed was not then founded. Yet, as time went on, though his careless way of living inflicted great tortures upon his much-abused tabernacle of flesh, he managed to obtain and retain the affection and even the respect of Calcutta, and when he left India for good and all, with a very small fortune, he departed amidst genuine tears. His last voyage home was as horrible, and is as well described as his other adventures by sea. He was welcomed by his two sisters, and for some years lived at Beaconsfield to be near his old friend, the widow of Edmund Burke. Of the last years of his life we know nothing.

In the Preface to this last volume we are told a little more about the manuscript of these Memoirs, information which, however belated, may be accepted as satisfactory. We are also told that the editor in reading the manuscript found many pages dull, and others which, owing to the freedom of Hickey's language, would be considered unfit for the choice ears of 1926. For these bad reasons 'the manuscript has gone through a process of elimination'. Later on in this Preface the editor holds out the hope of a new and unexpurgated edition 'fully annotated', and says: 'If such an edition should be contemplated, it would be essential that it should be prepared in collaboration by those who have made a special study of the life of the period, not only in England, but in India.' We trust this contemplated edition will some day appear, for no treatment can be too good for Hickey; and if the Notes and Annotations are confined either to the Margins or to Appendixes, all will be well for posterity. Happy is the man who has not yet read Hickey.

XVI

A CHURCH UNCHURCHED

XVI

A CHURCH UNCHURCHED

THE debates in Parliament in December 1927 on the proposals submitted by the late Archbishop of Canterbury in the name and on behalf of the Church of England to repeal the Act of Uniformity of 1662, so as to allow certain agreed modifications in the administration of her services, after beginning somewhat tamely in the Lords, where a large and favourable majority was easily secured, ended tumultuously in the Commons by the rejection of the proposals. The majority against the Church, though thirty-three in number, was, considering the importance of the occasion, not a large one, whilst the attendance in the division lobbies was curiously small.

This victory, perhaps an untoward event, would appear to be mainly due to the redoubtable man who has himself taught us to call 'Jix', thereby helping him to escape from the dull lists of 'double-barrelled mediocrities', into the loftier one of monosyllabic dignity—Pitt, Fox, Jix!

The victory was for the moment at all events a real one, for it cannot be denied by any student of ecclesiastical history that by the vote of Thursday, December 15, 1927, the Home Secretary in a

A CHURCH UNCHURCHED

Conservative Government has succeeded in unchurching the Church of England as by law established. It may be possible to retrace this step, but it will be difficult.

> 'Sed revocare gradum—
> Hoc opus, hic labor est.'

As it stands, what room is there now in the Established Church of England for Church principles, for the right, almost if not quite, the divine right of episcopacy and episcopal government; for the gift of the Holy Ghost descending upon the head of a Bishop on his consecration by the laying-on of the hands of three of his apostolically descended brethren? What need any longer to worry about the rule of faith, about sacramental gifts and graces, about authority as against private judgment, about antiquity, the early fathers, and the Four Councils? All these fine things go by the board in the Church of the Jixites. The lights of one of the three golden candlesticks have been blown out, and it is now made quite clear once for all that Macaulay was right when he stated in a head-note to his great Whig History that the Church of England originated at the Reformation.

Sir William Joynson-Hicks, like most great heresiarchs, was, unknown to himself, educated for the part history had destined him to play.

A CHURCH UNCHURCHED

Though not specially erudite, or seemingly marked out for an ecclesiastical career, we first hear of him as actively engaged in prosecuting a vigorous and well-endowed campaign against Anglo-Catholic views, and sending out paid missionaries into different parts of the country from whom he received, and sometimes did not receive, monthly reports of the success of their propaganda, and of the distribution of the truthful and temperate 'literature' with which he was careful to keep them well supplied.

On his part this was a labour of love, for all the time he was a prosperous and highly honourable solicitor of the High Court who found time not only to attend to the affairs of many private clients, but also to those of that democratic and truly comprehensive institution, the General Omnibus Company, which occasionally found itself in Court to meet the charge of running over stray foot-travellers—both Protestant and Papist—in the crowded streets of this great Metropolis.

Being thus fully equipped for his great task our Protestant leader had small difficulty in making a powerful oration against the Archbishop's proposals, in the course of which he made remarks with which many private citizens will agree, though most of them were irrelevant to the real issue before the House.

In the House of Lords Lord Davidson, then

the Archbishop of Canterbury, who knows his age, though not the House of Commons, as a schoolboy knows the contents of his pockets, introduced the repealing measure as composedly as if it were a Local Government Bill. He, indeed, hinted at the beginning that there were involved in his proposals some things that, were they gone into, would be found to touch upon the faith and devotional practices of such of his hearers as might chance to be Christians and Churchgoers, and not Jews, Nonconformists, and Agnostics, but he did this only to waive such things on one side as obviously out of place in their Lordships' House as at present constituted. After this hint his Grace went composedly on for an hour and ten minutes, during which he described the present plight of the Church and mildly inquired how best he and the Fathers in God around him were to get along in the future.

As I listened to this discourse, admirable and well-judged as I felt it to be, I could not but think of that 'great Achilles whom we knew', Mr. Gladstone; and of Roundell Palmer, of Lord Westbury and the saponaceous Samuel, of Robert Lowe and of that swashbuckling Erastian (of ecclesiastical descent), Sir William Harcourt; of the accumulated stores of their reading, of their intimate acquaintance with all the aspects of our Church history, of their fiery, if in some cases their

A CHURCH UNCHURCHED

unholy, zeal; and whilst half-asleep on the steps of the throne, I found myself murmuring Swinburne's lines to Walter Landor:—

> 'Come back in sleep, for in the life
> Where thou art not,
> We find none like thee.'

The laity in the Lords made no great figure. Lord Carson drew a picture for us of an old woman who loved her Prayer Book of 1662 because neither she nor her mother had ever heard of there ever having been any other Prayer Books, much less of the old Canon of the Mass to which her great-great-great-grandmothers were probably most fervently attached. Lord Carson's old lady, if left alone (so at least we all felt), would never discover that there was any difference between the so-called 'Deposited Book' and the one scheduled to the Act of 1662.

Lord Carson's picture did not prove to be a moving one, and was certainly below the level of Cowper's old woman, who:—

> 'Just knows, and knows no more, her Bible true,
> A truth the brilliant Frenchman never knew.'

When the measure got into the House of Commons a different spirit was at once manifested.

When Mr. Bridgeman, now ennobled, taking a leaf out of the Archbishop's book, said he was not going to discuss Christian doctrine, he was met with cries of 'Why not?' which discomposed him.

Why should not the representatives of the people discuss whatever they choose? Did not the Council of Nicæa discuss doctrine? It may be true that Nicæa was an Œcumenical Council and composed solely of clerics—but what of that? Are not our M.P.s the chosen vessels of democracy, and as well qualified to discuss theology as political economy?

Nevertheless, the point ought to have been made that the House of Commons, not being either an Œcumenical Council or a Church Synod, has no right to choose a creed for a Church or to arrange its services, but only to decide whether or not it will allow the seal of the State to be affixed to a Church that has by her proposals made it plain that she has ceased to represent the general religious sense of the nation.

The Cimmerian darkness that has apparently descended upon our ecclesiastical history seems to have prevented anybody in either House asking why in the name of conscience two thousand well-appointed divines in 1662 refused to give their 'unfeigned assent and consent to all and everything contained' in the Book Lord Carson's old woman loved so well; and sooner than do so were turned out to starve and die by the roadside.

A CHURCH UNCHURCHED

They may have been great fools for their pains, and many of them had during the Cromwellian usurpation ejected many equally conscientious divines for refusing to read the Directory of Public Worship—but still, out they went, and why?

For two reasons: *First*, because they saw, or thought they say, Rome in the new Prayer Book more clearly than in the second Prayer Book of King Edward the Sixth—not perhaps full-blooded Romanism, but the germs of it, and particularly in the Communion Service. Who can say they were wrong? Our Church Service has always been a compromise. As the great Lord Chatham expressed it, with its Calvinistic articles to please Geneva, its Romish liturgy to foster the seeds of its Catholicism, and its Arminian clergy to preach good works. Particularly was this accommodating spirit made plain in the Communion Service. The Altar and the Table with its 'fair white cloth' were alike admitted into the parish church. The Table for Commemoration and the Altar for sacrifice, each has as much, or as little, right to be there as the other.

During the eighteenth century the Table theory may have prevailed over the Altar theory, though even in what Mr. Gladstone used to call, with a shudder, 'the bad times' of Bishop Hoadly and Archdeacon Paley, there were always bishops, priests, and laymen to uphold the Altar and the

A CHURCH UNCHURCHED

Descent of the Holy Spirit on the Elements after consecration by a priest.

Of late years Church principles have spread, reaching even so far as St. Giles', Edinburgh. Low Church views, like those entertained by the late Miss Catherine Marsh, have suffered an eclipse since the days when the late Lord Lincolnshire was first taken to the Chapel Royal by his mother and almost dedicated to fight for the Cause that far-seeing lady already perceived to be in danger.

The Deposited Book is as much a compromise as its predecessors, but it is a compromise slightly in favour of the Altar. Doctrinally, we are assured there is no difference. Certainly there is none Romewards, though some keen noses have detected a step in the direction of the Eastern Church. All dogmas are mostly matters of emphasis. The Church of Rome is as evangelical as ever was the late Charles Simeon, but she also places emphasis on Church authority and so on all through the Creeds.

The other reason why many people of light and leading became and remained Nonconformists was because they kicked at episcopacy.

Why did John Knox, the author of that Black Rubric so many lovers of the Prayer Book have just discovered, refuse the English Bishopric that was offered him? Why did Richard Baxter say *Nolo Episcopari*? Why did Doddridge? Simply because they thought there was no certain warrant in Holy Scripture for episcopacy. Jix and his friends have no such squeamish scruples. They have no objection to the order of Bishops so long as there is no need to pay any attention to them.

The Home Secretary has dreams of a Federation (within the State) of Protestant Churches. Has he ever considered the question of Holy Orders? Probably not.